the necessity of certain behaviors

Drue Heinz Literature Prize 2011

the necessity of certain behaviors

Shannon Cain

University of Pittsburgh Press

Published by the University of Pittsburgh Press, Pittsburgh, Pa., 15260
Copyright © 2011, Shannon Cain
All rights reserved
Manufactured in the United States of America
Printed on acid-free paper

10 9 8 7 6 5 4 3 2 1

Library of Congress Cataloging-in-Publication Data
Cain, Shannon.
The necessity of certain behaviors / Shannon Cain.
p. cm. -- (Drue Heinz literature prize 2011)
ISBN 978-0-8229-4410-2 (cloth : acid-free paper)
I. Title.
PS3603.A389N43 2011
813'.6--dc22
                                    2011021270

for Brennan

contents

the necessity of certain behaviors

this is how it starts

there is a boy and there is a girl. Jane sees the girl on Tuesdays and Fridays and she sees the boy on Wednesdays and Saturdays. The other three nights she sleeps by herself in her big, firm bed.

She gathers the dogs each morning at six. This requires both the boy and the girl to leave her apartment and refrain from preparing her breakfast. Given the chance, the boy would make eggs benedict. The girl would make cheese omelets. On Jane's mornings alone, she eats cold cereal with sugar.

The girl is fond of her strap-on. The boy is fond of cunnilingus. This is satisfying to Jane. Plus, Jane can say this to the girl: "It would be nice if your dick were bigger." Jane would not make this statement to the boy, though it may be slightly true.

Jane goes to art school in the afternoons and walks dogs six mornings a week and again at night. She realizes this is a cliché, the student dog-walker, but such is her life and she can't help it. She lives in an apartment that has been occupied since 1948 by a member of her immediate family. In New York, you treat rent control like an heirloom.

Outside her window there are identical brick buildings surrounding a courtyard with mature elms and a well-maintained playground. Jane grew up on those swings. Twenty-five thousand people in a half-mile radius live in apartments identical to Jane's, with their metal kitchen cabinets and square pedestal sinks in the bathrooms. She is comforted by this sameness, and by her place inside it. Eight years ago, Jane's mother moved to Boca Raton in a nest emptying role-reversal, as per family tradition. Unless Jane produces a child, the corporation that owns the buildings will quadruple the rent when she moves out. Her mother takes for granted that Jane will prevent this from happening. So, she supposes, does Jane.

The girl often gets lost in the maze of buildings when she comes to see Jane. She calls from her cell phone. "I'm at a fountain," she says. Sometimes there's no landmark other than a mound of daffodils. Jane comes down to find her.

The girl is a doctor. The boy is a lawyer. If they were married to one another they'd have kids who resent their ambition. They'd live in Upper Montclair and commute to Manhattan. The boy, in fact, does live in Upper Montclair. The boy is someone's father but the girl isn't anyone's mother. Jane is not necessarily reminded of her own mother when she looks at the girl, but nevertheless the girl frowns in a disapproving way from time to time that makes Jane feel like lying to her.

Jane calls the girl at the hospital and says she'd like to play nurse. The girl is a feminist and reminds Jane that patriarchal power trips do not turn her on. Jane takes the number six train uptown and waits for the girl in her office, and when the girl's shift is over Jane crawls under the desk and performs some oral tricks she learned from the boy.

In his law office on East 52nd Street, the boy represents children with chronic health conditions caused by lousy medical treatment. Jane doesn't know how he can bear to spend so much of his day with heartbroken people.

The girl is shorter than Jane and has beautiful breasts. They are small and oval, with very pink nipples. A tuft of turquoise hair sprouts from the left side of her head, and her ears have many piercings. Her eyeglass frames came from the 26th Street flea market. In the emergency room where she works, teenage patients tell her their secrets. It is not uncommon, she tells Jane, for adults to ask for a different doctor. Despite Jane's status as an art student and its accompanying expectation of hipness, she cannot match the girl's effortless bohemian chic.

The boy is tall. He has two children, a son and a daughter. They attend a private Montessori school on the Upper West Side. His daughter plays the oboe in a junior symphony, which is unusual for a child of eight. His son plays soccer, which is not unusual for a child of any age. Sometimes Jane goes to Upper Montclair on Sunday afternoons to watch the boy's son run around the field with other four-year-olds. The boy's enthusiasm for his son's team is endearing. When the boy spots his ex-wife at the game, he puts his arm around Jane's shoulders.

In her big, firm bed, the boy is huge, a 240-pound sandbag. Jane likes the feel of his heaviness; likes to know she can handle the weight of his body without gasping for air. On Fridays, the girl, who is considerate about such things, brings paraphernalia in different sizes. She is a hundred pounds lighter than the boy.

The girl and the boy know about one another. Jane sometimes considers introducing them. The next part of this fantasy involves Jane floating a proposal that they both occupy her bed, maybe on Thursdays and Sundays. Jane knows the girl would not go for this. The boy, it goes nearly without saying, would.

The boy surprises Jane with expensive tickets to see a famous lesbian comedian. The show is on a Tuesday, which is the girl's night. Jane calls the girl.

"I need to reschedule," Jane says.

"This is how it starts," the girl says.

Jane's apartment has two bedrooms. In New York, this is sometimes more space than entire families occupy. She makes her art in the spare bedroom, painting on panes of glass purchased at the hardware store. The paintings are meant to be viewed in reverse, through the smooth surface of the glass. To accomplish this, she must paint her foregrounds first, top layers before bottom. She must put the blush on a cheek before she paints the cheek. Sometimes she sits for an hour, looking out the window at her slivered view of the East River, planning her layers.

Jane has always been this way with boys and girls. She likes boys for their size and for their crudeness, the way they bumble through life thinking they're in control. She loves girls for their strength but mostly for their skill in the sack. She doesn't like the way that girls talk so much, the way they sit and talk cross-legged and shirtless on the couch or sit and talk in the recliner by the window or sit and talk on the bed, straddling Jane.

The girl is a talker. Often when the talking mood strikes the girl, her lips are pink and maybe still slightly puffy from her vigorous interaction with Jane's. Jane makes sounds to signify that she's listening.

Jane's mother calls from her duplex in Florida. She wants Jane to find a photo of her grandfather she believes is located in a cardboard box in the hall closet. Jane conducts the search holding the phone with her shoulder. Dust stirs.

"The house next door finally sold," her mother says, "to a couple of women."

"I'm not finding it, Ma," Jane says.

"Don't make me come look for it myself!"

In her retirement, Jane's mother has become a smart aleck.

"I hope you aren't harassing them," Jane says.

"They told me they're cousins. Such bullshit. Seventy-year-old cousins buying a house together? What do they think, I'm Anita Bryant?"

"The picture isn't here," Jane says, and sneezes. "They're afraid. Bring them a cake."

"God bless. With a frosting yoni, how about."

Jane is the only dog walker in the eleven thousand identical apartments outside her window. Her mother started the business when Jane was seven years old. The complex has an economy of its own, a closed system, of which Jane is a part. Hardware stores nearby sell fans that go neatly in the small horizontal windows, shelves that fit in the dead space between the coat closet and the front door, replacement kitchen cabinet knobs. Jane does the math: there are 198,000 cabinet knobs in her complex.

Jane has twenty-five dog-walking clients. She takes the first group at six a.m. and the next at eight. She repeats the pattern at four p.m. and again at six. The dogs are grateful. The humans are in fact technically her clients, but she knows she works for the animals. She picks up the dogs' warm shit only because they can't do it for themselves.

"Let me come to work with you," the boy says. His kids are at their mother's house. It's a bright Sunday and the boy's lips are still slippery from his adventure down below and she feels in no position to deny him. They get dressed and fetch the dogs.

In each building's lobby, he holds the leashes while she runs upstairs to collect more clients. This makes the work go faster. "I'll leave the law," he says, "and be your doggie boy." His hair stands up in back, pillow-mussed. The bill of his baseball cap is frayed, the cardboard showing through. His T-shirt says *Vito's Pork Shop*. He hasn't yet shaved.

"No you won't," Jane says.

"Dare me." He pants a little, sticking out the tip of his tongue.

"The pay is lousy, my friend," Jane says. She takes the leashes from his hand and pushes past him, to the next building.

The boy walks behind her, all the dogs at her side. There is silence, during which she assumes his thoughts have moved on to football or food. But at the next doorway he says, "Lousy pay is why they invented rent control." His eyes flicker upward, in the direction of her apartment.

In evolutionary terms, her job at this moment is to encourage him. Her girl instinct is clear about this. She is supposed to say something to spark further comments regarding shared domesticity.

To make her art, Jane is required to know everything about the image before she starts painting. She cannot paint a table then put an orange on it later. She must paint the orange first and then form the table around it. She enjoys the puzzle of this technique. Her teacher frowns at her work. He says if she insists on preventing the painting from emerging of its own accord, her art will have no depth. He cannot see that flatness is the entire point. She will probably fail his class.

The girl does not appreciate animals. This is unusual for a lesbian. She plants her bare feet in Jane's kitchen and prepares a vegetable upside-down cake with organic carrots and fresh dill and basil. Jane drinks wine at the dinette table left behind when her grandmother moved to Phoenix in 1981 and watches the girl through the kitchen doorway. The fluorescent lighting makes the girl's short blonde hair glow like the wood fairy in a picture book belonging to the boy's oboe-playing daughter.

The girl scoffs at Jane's paltry collection of spices.

"I've survived so far with no sage in my life," Jane replies.

The girl removes her blouse and finishes her cookery performing an impersonation of Emeril on ecstasy, topless. Jane pours more wine for the girl and holds the glass to her lips. She is wildly attracted to feminine women with an edge.

"I love you," says the boy.
"I love you," says the girl.

The boy has purchased a society-building computer game for his daughter. The child constructs a virtual room with no doors and places her avatar inside. The avatar pees in the corner. She grows depressed and lonely. After two weeks she curls up and dies. The boy makes an appointment with a child psychologist, who advises him to ask his daughter how much she really enjoys the oboe. As he tells this story to Jane, he cries.

The girl has deeply green eyes. She asks Jane to leave the boy. She says this, and then is silent. Against this self-assuredness the boy doesn't stand a chance. Lying in the girl's arms, Jane should be thinking about what to say next, but she ponders instead the unfair advantage of girls over boys. Their adaptable body parts and their ability to say what they mean. She falls into a bewildered silence.

In the subway car, the boy sits with his knees spread apart. Jane compensates by pressing her legs together, sideways. Other men on the train sit this way, too. She points it out to the boy. "It's a physical thing," he says into her ear. "One mustn't constrict the package." Also the boy has a loud voice. He doesn't mean to occupy all that aural space, but it happens. Often she feels a great need to tell him to pipe down, especially in restaurants.

She calls the girl at the hospital to cancel their Tuesday. "I'm sick," Jane says. "I think it's the flu."

"Drink fluids," the girl says. Being a girl and a doctor, she knows a lie.

"I'll see you next week," Jane says.

The girl doesn't say anything more. The girl is figuring her out.

Jane's clothing accumulates on the floor around her bed. At six a.m., she roots through the pile for jeans and a T-shirt. There is a faint smell of dog shit. She collects the dirty pants and shirts and piles them into the wicker laundry basket that has lived in the hall closet since before she was born. When members of her family abandon the apartment, they buy new household items upon arrival in their retirement communities. She imagines her grandmother breezily pushing a modern lightweight iron over her housedresses. Serving poolside cocktails in tropical drinkware made of plastic. Objects in Jane's kitchen have vintage value: a mirrored toaster shaped like an egg, a set of Flintstones jelly-jar glasses, a pale yellow Fiesta Ware butter dish.

The laundry room in the basement is empty. She pushes quarters into the slots and starts a load. When Jane was twelve, her mother sent her downstairs to bring up the whites and she walked in to find a man she recognized from the elevator fucking a woman who wasn't his wife. The woman sat on the washer containing the bed sheets Jane had come to collect. It made a vibrating, spin-cycle racket. With great earnestness the man pumped away, his pants around his ankles. The woman's blouse was off her shoulder, her skirt bunched around her waist. Her head was thrown back, an unselfconscious expression on her face. Jane stayed rooted to the cement floor, looking at the woman. "Run along, now, honey," the woman said to her, and smiled. She panted, as though she'd been running. She didn't cover herself or jump off the washer. Jane smiled back and went outside and sat on the swings.

She leaves her laundry to its cycles and collects her clients from their sleepy owners. She walks them through the silent green grounds between the red brick buildings. There is so little sky in the city.

It is part of her routine to leave the kitchen light on so she can find her window from outside. She notices the harshness of the fluorescent bulb, and the way that her window stands apart from the others. She's supposed to walk the dogs briskly, give them some exercise. She is aware that some of the owners watch from their windows. She sits on a bench outside the playground where in the third grade she kissed Sissy Hirshfeld. It was St. Patrick's Day, and Sissy had a four-leaf clover painted on her cheek. Sissy's brother, Donny, whose Valentine to Jane had a picture of Minnie and Mickey Mouse holding hands, watched them.

Jane is painting a pair of women on barstools. One wears red sneakers. She hasn't done the background yet, but when she does it will be an outdoor scene, with a river flowing behind them and dark clouds in the distance. The woman being watched has heavy-lidded eyes, which Jane didn't intend. She was going for a detached gaze, but has ended up making her look sleepy. She works on the figure in red sneakers, who seems to have lost interest in participating in the scene. She looks like she'd prefer a naked run along the beach. Jane stares at the picture for thirty-eight minutes. She finds a pair of pliers in the drawer and using the handle cracks the glass neatly in half with one firm tap. The two heads look out at her. One is distracted, the other just tired.

The boy buys Jane a puppy. It is inordinately cute. "What am I supposed to do with this?" Jane says.

The boy is crestfallen. "How can you deny this face?" he says, cradling the dog. "She's purebred. She's smart."

"I have plenty of animals in my life already," she says.

"But you love dogs," he tells her.

"Other people's," she says, and kisses him. He's just come from work; his tie is loosened. She pets the short hair at the back of his neck. He puts the dog down and carries Jane to the kitchen, where he plops her on the counter and removes her jeans. Over his shoulder Jane watches the puppy sniff around the closet door, where she keeps leashes and poop bags. The puppy whines and scratches at the floor. The boy moans. Jane thinks about the girl.

At two o'clock in the morning, Jane's doorbell rings. The boy is sound asleep in Jane's big, firm bed.

"How did you get into the building?" Jane asks the girl.

"I fucked the doorman," the girl says.

"There is no doorman," Jane says.

"I have something for you," the girl says, grinning seductively. "In here." She brandishes a leather backpack, and eyes the closed bedroom door.

"You're a little bit drunk, aren't you?" Jane says.

From inside the bathroom, the puppy scratches. Jane lets him out and he bounds over to the girl, butt wiggling. The girl doesn't bend over. "What's this?"

"I'm not keeping it," Jane says.

"It's cute," the girl says. "Maybe I'll take it home."

"You hate animals."

"I'm starting to come around. What's it called?"

"A golden retriever."

"I know that much. What's its name?"

"Untitled," Jane says. "You don't want this dog."

"Why not?" the girl says. She hasn't touched it. "It's growing on me already."

"For one," Jane says, "it's a boy dog."

"And for two?"

"For two." Jane pauses. "I haven't decided whether to keep it yet."

"I thought so," the girl says.

They sit together on the couch. It's a small couch, upholstered in horses and carriages and ladies in hoop skirts. Their knees are touching. The puppy slinks to the corner. The girl puts her hands over her face and cries. Jane hadn't expected this.

"You aren't sick," the girl says. She takes her damp hands from her face and puts them on either side of Jane's neck. "Your glands aren't even swollen." Her voice is louder than usual.

"I'm sorry," Jane says.

The girl looks at her through red eyes. The girl begins to talk. In her speech there are references to needs, to respect, to truth. She talks for nine minutes. The clock on the VCR is just over the girl's shoulder. The girl curls and uncurls the strap on her backpack. She winds down with a mention of survival, then intimacy. Jane watches her face, which is beautiful.

There is a pause, during which Jane does what she always does when the girl finishes talking. She searches for something relevant to say, some piece of information, something that will not require her to form a sentence containing any of the same words the girl has just used. She looks for a small fact, a clarification. What she ends up with is this: "The dog was a gift."

"Ah," the girl says.

"I'm giving it back," Jane says.

"Don't," the girl says. "Give it to me." She glances at the bedroom door. "I dare you."

"You don't want this dog."

Outside, a window across the courtyard goes dark.

"Right," the girl says, and leaves.

"I'm going back to my wife," the boy says. They are sitting at the dinette table. Normally he would be gone by the end of her first dog shift but today she comes home to eggs on the table.

She pushes her plate away. "This is my great-grandmother's china. It's antique."

"It was on the top shelf," he says. He gestures vaguely toward the kitchen.

"Don't tell me," Jane says. "It's for the sake of the children."

"Right, that's about right."

"Yeah. You owe it to them."

"No need to get bitchy, Jane. I needed to do this"—he gestures to the space between them—"to figure myself out."

"Glad to be of service."

The boy stands, picks up the puppy. "You never really wanted him."

"No," she finally says. The dog licks his plate. "Give it to the kids."

"Jill is allergic."

"Jill. Christ. What's your mother's name? June?"

"All right, then." He puts the puppy down and takes their plates to the kitchen. "Say what you will. I deserve it, I guess."

It's a trick of the modern boy, Jane thinks. Show us the best of yourself on the way out the door.

"So the dog was a consolation prize."

He stands in the kitchen doorway. "I get it," he says. "You're pissed."

She stands up and removes her pants. "I'm getting in the shower." She moves toward the bathroom. With her back to him she takes off her shirt, then her underwear. She does not turn to face him. "Do the dishes before you leave. Chip a plate and I'm giving my grandmother your phone number."

She sits on the bathroom floor, which is chilly against her naked skin. It is tiled with ceramic octagons the size of a quarter. They need re-grouting. Oyster crackers, she thinks they're called. While she waits for him to leave she does the math: in the bathrooms of her apartment complex there are 3.2 million oyster crackers.

She must turn in something for art class, which won't do much good for her grade but will at least represent having taken a stand against professorial interference. In her newest painting, a woman in a black cocktail dress sits on a large empty box in the middle of a prairie. She is barefoot. The prairie grasses are long, and bent by the wind. In the distance are fat white clouds. The woman's head is thrown back, taking in the sun. Her legs hang over the side of the box, whose black interior is the only stillness around.

Jane rents a storage room roughly the size of her kitchen in a twelve-story building near the docks on the West Side. The location is inconvenient, which is probably for the best. The hallways are carpeted and lined with padlocked doors. The view from the stairwell window is magnificent. She wonders how many years it will take for the owners to install plumbing and rent the units as studio apartments.

She calls a moving company, which sends two large men to her apartment. They take away her grandmother's table, the couch, the boxes in the closet. She wraps the jelly glasses and the china in newspaper and packs them in a wooden crate. The men haul it all away, wordlessly. Vacated by her mother's needlepoint, the walls are spotted with clean squares. Jane's footsteps echo. She puts her mattress in the middle of the bedroom floor and hangs her art in the living room windows. Through the painted glass, the light throws muddy, deformed images against the bare parquet tiles.

After two weeks the girl hasn't called. Jane is pregnant. She calls her mother, who is pragmatic about such things.

"You're not ready," her mother says. "Live a little, I say. I'm sending money. I'm doing it now." Jane can hear her mother licking the envelope. "Don't go to the place in Queens, whatever you do. Helen from 4C went there and the nurses were bitchy."

Jane sits on the kitchen counter with the phone to her ear and is silent. Her mother talks, filling up space, which is good.

"Call the doctor," her mother says.

At first Jane doesn't know what she means. There's a silence. "She isn't in the picture anymore, Ma."

"I'm walking to the mailbox with this check," her mother says.

"How about you bring it here yourself?" Jane says.

Jane is pretty sure her mother is crying. "Tell the doctor you need her, is my advice. She'll come along, she'll drive you home afterward, feed you soup." Jane hears her mother's footsteps on the gravel driveway. She pictures an open sky and palm trees.

cultivation

One evening, Maury calls. Those public service announcements, he tells Frances, the ones about casual drug consumption supporting terrorism? Apparently they're working. Now his customers insist *their* marijuana be grown domestically. He needs the entirety of her last two harvests, which Frances estimates at roughly twelve pounds, counting the supply that's now curing in Mason jars in her basement. "These people buy organic produce, if you know what I mean," Maury says. "They read the *New York Times.*"

He'll pay her a thousand dollars a pound, but he wants her to deliver it. Here's the trouble: Memphis is fifteen hundred miles from Phoenix, and her three kids are home from school for the summer.

At the dinner table, Frances says, "How about a road trip?"

The boys throw their hands in the air, cheering her. Todd, the six-year-old, her little sports freak, the kid whose Little League coach is already planning his career, wants to know if they can sleep in a tent. The middle one, Robbie, who is eight and plays chess and computer games, says he guesses Memphis is cool. Emily inches one shoulder toward her ear, a half-shrug that is one of her few signals of approval. Emily is fourteen.

Frances doesn't grow pot because she's a desperate single mother, though she is. She grows it to pay off her half of the forty thousand dollars in credit card debt she and her ex racked up during their marriage. Recently her minimum payments have become unreasonable. On three separate credit cards, the Amount Due squats resolutely above the ten thousand dollar mark, unaffected by the enormous sums she sends each month. At 19 percent interest, she figures, Todd will have graduated from college before she pays off the debt. She'll still be wringing payments from her meager take-home as a per diem nurse on the oncology ward, digging herself fruitlessly deeper into the hole. In the memo line of her checks, she scrawls her account number followed by *you fuckers*, an act that offers diminishing satisfaction with each new check. Lately she's had to rotate payments; she pays one bill, neglects the next. A shift in tone has occurred in the personalized notes printed on her bills: they've evolved from the tactful supposition of Frances's forgetfulness to the sinister hint of third-party collections.

So there's the money. Yet, also: there's nothing else in her life that offers the same satisfaction as the squat plants, the cultivation of perfect, tight, and tender buds, the recognition that she's expert at something. She grows weed and she grows children, but the weed doesn't talk back. The children make noise and messes. The weed is reliable. She feeds, she prunes, she waters, and uncomplicated as the sunrise, it grows.

Some of it she smokes, but who needs that much pot? She reaps three ounces per square foot every sixteen weeks, a yield right up there with the big guys. The plants fill a walk-in closet in the basement she's double-deadbolted against Emily, a kid who emerged from Frances's womb demanding to know everything.

Frances uses the Screen of Green method, which requires careful attention to the training of each plant for maximum light on the buds and involves a complicated system of chicken wire, drip irrigation, grow lights, air flow fans, irrigation tubes, water pumps, thermostats, and exhaust pipes. Industrial-grade soundboard and weatherstripping ensure all this activity goes undiscovered by Emily. If she suspects anything, she hasn't mentioned it.

The promise of a cross-country adventure has excited the boys, requiring more bedtime parenting than usual. When all three are finally asleep, Frances goes to the basement to smoke her excellent pot, empties the dehumidifier in her drying cabinet, then pads barefoot to their bedsides and stands over their sleeping bodies. She bends close to their faces to peer at them in the dark. The eyelashes! The lips! She wanders from bedroom to bedroom. Their faces are never, during the day, as still as this. Emily's scowl is absent; she looks like she did in kindergarten, before Frances married the boys' father. Emily would hate to know her mother stares at her like this, big teenage girl that she is; she'd accuse Frances of invading her privacy. Frances absorbs the impossible beauty of her children. She gets teary with the joy of their existence and the delirium of primo homegrown.

The day before their trip, Frances purchases an aerodynamic cargo carrier and a serious padlock. Inside the garage, she straps it to the top of the minivan and packs it with cardboard boxes of clothes the boys have outgrown and toys they've ignored for months. Together with these items she places two small nylon duffel bags purchased on sale at Target, one decorated with retro daisies and the other with soccer balls. Each contains six vacuum-sealed packages that weigh one pound each. She stayed up most of the night before with her vacuum sealer (purchased last year via infomercial), sucking the air out of Ziploc freezer bags and wrapping them in duct tape. She closes the carrier and walks around the car, sniffing.

The next morning she assembles her children in the driveway. On the front lawn, the boys are engaged in a vigorous game of Slug Bug, undaunted by an absence of Volkswagens on their street.

Emily points to the cargo carrier. "What's in there?"

"Empty!" Frances says. "In case we want to do some shopping. In Memphis."

"We have malls here, Mom," Emily says.

Frances lets her gaze fall to Emily's torso. "What is that you're wearing? Some sort of dress, or what?" Some mornings it appears to Frances as if Emily's breasts have become larger as she slept. "Never mind," Frances tells her. "Come on, boys, let's hit the road."

In the car there are significant stretches of quiet. There is so much to see through the windows. Emily and the boys have their heads down, occupied with books or GameBoys or DVDs. Frances is struck with melancholy that no one in the car is in diapers anymore.

"You're missing this country!" she says. "Look outside, kids!" They must be climbing in altitude, for the landscape has become a hybrid of prairie and desert, long grass dotted with cholla cacti. Winds that don't seem to know which direction they're headed whip the grasses flat in great wide swaths of motion, exposing white underbellies, then toss them upright, green again. Given all the gusting energy outside, it strikes Frances as strange that the interior of the minivan is so utterly without breeze. How completely a person can be insulated. "Look, guys!" she says. "Look how the grass is like waves!" Three blonde heads turn to the left. Six green eyes register a view that fails to hold their interest.

"That's real nice, Mom," Emily says. She's reading *Herland* by Charlotte Perkins Gilman.

"Yeah, Mom, real nice!" yells Todd.

Frances remains silent for ten or twelve miles until Todd informs her it's time to stop for lunch and besides he needs to poop. This sets off a round of butt jokes. From the back of her throat Emily offers a loud sigh.

"They can't help it," Frances tells her.

"Twerps," Emily says. "Brain-damaged cockroaches."

"Later on you'll love them," Frances says.

"Extremely doubtful," Robbie says. Robbie was named, regrettably, after his father. It was still in the first year of Frances's marriage to him, even as she suspected the guy was fucking Emily's soccer coach. The little twerp won't let Frances call him Bob, Robert, or even Bobby. Todd, on the other hand, was a save-the-marriage baby, a fact for which she is only now on the verge of forgiving herself, thanks to expensive biweekly therapy.

At the Burger King in Gallup, Emily studies the carrier and says, "Why don't we put the suitcases in there? We'd have more room inside the van."

"Plenty of room all around, sweetie," Frances says. Todd is grabbing for Robbie's milkshake, held maddeningly by Robbie out of short arms' range. Todd's face has that pre-eruption expression. It's evoked so often by Robbie that Frances suspects he's trying for a record: how many times in one day can he make his brother wail in frustration? "Whoa, little dude," Frances says, and steers him toward the minivan. "You don't want that anyhow. Cooties on the straw and such."

Todd wiggles in satisfaction. He'll take the comment as evidence she loves him more than she does his brother. Which isn't true, of course. Before the boys were born she couldn't bear the thought of loving another child the way she did Emily. But there they were, and she does. She searches the rearview mirror to give Robbie a wink but he won't meet her eye.

Frances needs to make a decision about lying to Emily. The kid's inquisitive nature has been bolstered lately by a sharpening sense of logic—that's what Frances gets, she realizes ruefully, for sending Emily and the boys to decent schools—and an increasingly distrustful outlook on the world in general. Either Frances has to get much craftier about her basement activity or she needs to give up the deception entirely and tell Emily everything.

But it's the job of a mother to reveal truths to her children in increments they can handle. Last year when some kid on the playground called Robbie a math dweeb and he came home wanting to know what that meant, Frances didn't tell him about pocket protectors and rejection by girls and how high school is hell for kids like him. She told him only enough so he understood that the kid who called him that name was confused and jealous and sad. Emily, though, is getting to the age when subtleties are important. At some point soon, Frances is going to need to explain to her that the stuff they're teaching her in school about drugs ignores important shades of gray. As it is, she's learning there's pretty much no difference between pot and crystal meth. Frances would like to tell the zealots that champion the D.A.R.E. curriculum—the cops and vice principals of the world—about the cancer patients on her ward. How grateful the family members are when she pulls them aside in the hallway and tells them she can get them top-grade marijuana to ease the unbearable, humiliating nausea and build the appetites of their loved ones. How, handing her a hundred bucks—a substantial discount—for a baggie containing twenty joints, they sometimes cry with relief and gratitude. They hug her, the big, suffering hugs of people whose nightmares are unfolding before them, and they tell her she's an angel. That God should bless her.

Robbie, on the other hand, would take in stride the truth about her basement endeavors. For a few miles, Frances engages in a fantasy in which she and her grown-up son work together in a mother-son business. She'd do the cultivating; Robbie, his gift for numbers honed in Advanced Placement math and an MBA from Yale, would handle the management side.

She looks at him in the mirror on the back of her visor. He is quietly placing tiny wads of chewed-up paper in Todd's hair.

"Emily," Frances says.

Emily sighs and saves her page with her finger.

"The cargo carrier," Frances whispers. "It's not empty."

"I knew it." Emily smiles. It's so easy, Frances thinks. Their trust is always there, right at the surface, waiting.

"I'm giving a bunch of your brothers' old things away." She looks behind her, unnecessarily. "You remember Maury, my friend from college? He lives in Memphis now and he has a son and I told him I'd bring them some toys and clothes. Don't tell Todd and Robbie."

"Just as long as you don't try to give away Todd's baseball stuff," Emily says, her voice low. She opens her book and smiles into it.

Frances's supply of cheap tricks cannot, apparently, be exhausted.

There is no shortage of law enforcement patrolling the American interstate system. Emily has empowered herself with a range of front-seat responsibilities, one of which is monitoring Frances's speed. "It's a construction zone, Mom," she says. "Fifty-five."

Normally Frances would arch an eyebrow and remind her who's the mother here, but she figures for the sake of harmony she can swallow a little teenage interference. At home, Emily digs through the recycling bin to make sure each of the yogurt containers bears a number two triangle symbol. When the electric bill arrives in a pink envelope, the sign that it's overdue, she pulls it from the stack of mail spilling out of the wicker basket on the countertop—the basket Emily organizes on a regular basis, throwing out junk and sorting bills by their due date—and shakes it at Frances accusingly. "How can you *forget* to pay a bill, Mom? How is that *possible?*" Once Frances came home from work early and found Emily at the kitchen counter, frowning over a stack of credit card statements.

The genetic source of all this angst is a mystery: like Frances, Emily's father—whom Frances hasn't seen since she was nineteen and pregnant— wasn't especially concerned about fiscal responsibility. She never knew him well enough to understand whether Emily's neuroses could have come from his side of the family. It doesn't much matter, though: Frances long ago gave up the struggle to get Emily to relax and act like a kid.

Given the odds, given a 1500-mile road trip with the distraction of the boys in the backseat, it is bound to happen, and it does, in the early afternoon of day two, just west of Amarillo. Emily sees the flashing lights first. "Mom! Oh my God, it's a police car *right* behind us! What were you doing, ninety? Mom, he's pulling you over. Pull over! I can't *believe* this!"

"Emily, honey. It's just a cop." She does wish, though, that they weren't in Texas.

"What about that ticket when I was in sixth grade? You got points on your driver's license, didn't you? How many will you have now? I swear to God, if you lose your license my life is ruined."

"Deep breaths, sweetheart. Not a big deal. Not the end of the universe." She looks in the rearview mirror. The cop hasn't yet emerged from his car.

"Mom's in trouble!" Robbie sings.

"Shut up, butthead," Emily says. She's already going after her fingernails. Frances cranes her neck to check on Todd. His mouth is in a serious line, his little forehead furrowed. "It's okay, lovey," Frances says. "Mommy was just driving a little too fast. I guess."

The cop is friendly enough. Emily looks straight ahead and grips her armrests. Frances had, it turns out, not seen a sign that required slowing down for a high wind area. Not able to miss the action, Robbie rolls down his window. The cop looks in the backseat. "How's it going, boys?" he says. They squeak out a couple of tiny *okays*. They're such little ones, Frances thinks.

He hands her the citation. "What're you carrying up top?" he says.

"Just luggage," she says. "Camping stuff." She puts her hand near her jaw to hide the throbbing of blood through her jugular vein, then realizes touching your face is nervous body language and places it casually, she hopes, on the steering wheel.

"Look out for these winds," he says. "Sometimes these carriers can throw off your balance. A gust hits the car sideways and the extra height makes things tricky." He gives the carrier a knock with his knuckles. "Especially in these minivans. Slow down, ma'am. Have a nice day, kids."

They find a campground east of Oklahoma City called Lake Eufaula. The boys indulge in another series of irritating wordplay jokes. Frances finds a spot near the water's edge, uncomfortably far from the parking lot, up an embankment, but at least a distance away from a family of speed-boaters and a group of spirited college-age students with a huge cooler. She decides not to worry about leaving the weed in the carrier overnight. The boys attempt to pitch the tent, give up and spend two hours smearing themselves with mud from the bottom of the lake, washing it off and smearing again. Frances and Emily figure out the tent stakes and poles and loops. They all roast hot dogs and marshmallows and Frances wishes her father were alive to meet his fine grandsons. They could use a grandpa, to play chess with Robbie and catch with Todd. She resolves to learn how to fish, to take them to a pond someday, give them poles and worms. She waits until she's sure the kids are asleep—the boys go down fast and solid but Emily tosses for a while—before she lights a joint and melts into campfire and stars and the lap of lake water.

In the middle of the night, she wakes up to Emily groping around in the dark. "Where's the flashlight?" Emily whispers. "I have to pee."

"Damn, honey. I left it in the car," Frances says. "My keys—"

"They're in your jeans pocket," Emily tells her. The moonlight makes the tent nylon glow green. Frances finds her jeans, crumpled in the corner of the tent, and hands the keys to Emily. "It's in the far back—"

"I know where it is," Emily says, and zips her way out the door.

"Can you see? Is it too dark?"

"I'm all *right*, Mom."

The boys are asleep on their sides, mouths open, Robbie's eyeballs active under his lids. Frances thinks about Emily making her way through the dark campground, considers climbing out of her sleeping bag to go with her to the cinderblock toilet structure. You never know when drunken college boys are lurking in the woods. Her mattress is softening from air loss, but she's still comfortable and sleepy and doesn't particularly want to get up. In the distance she hears the chirp of the minivan's alarm disengaging. Two weeks ago, doing the laundry, Frances found a letter from Emily to her most recent best friend, Breanne. It described a moment after band practice with a boy named Miguel wherein Emily's breasts were touched. Only the top half, her perfectly tidy handwriting was careful to note: no nipple.

That hardly counts, Frances found herself thinking. When Frances was twelve, her sixteen-year-old cousin Henry grabbed her breasts at an Easter picnic, zeroing in and twisting, and in return Frances whacked him on the temple with the hard edge of a tennis racket, a move that got her in huge trouble, given that the injury over which she retaliated had left no evidence of equal harm.

Emily's letter indicated nothing about the incident with Miguel being non-consensual, a fact about which Frances feels both relief and foreboding. Her therapist later informed her that fourteen-year-old girls do not leave notes to their friends in the pockets of their jeans unless they're trying to tell their mothers something.

Wide awake, she waits for her heart to come back to her from the dark woods. Finally she hears Emily's footsteps. "Sweetie?" she whispers. "Is that you?" Frances unzips her bag, gropes for her shoes and leaves the tent. Emily is standing at the edge of the water.

"Hey, baby," Frances says. "Not tired?"

"Todd was snoring," she says. "I rolled him over but then I couldn't get back to sleep."

"What are you doing with your backpack?" Frances says.

"I was going to sit here and read." She shrugs. "Only the flashlight just died."

"Rats," Frances says.

"Why did you lie to that cop?" Emily says.

Frances sighs. She's still feeling the effects of her bedtime joint. "I couldn't exactly tell him the truth in front of the boys. Plus cops are always suspicious. He'd only have kept us sitting there longer, asking questions."

"Yeah, all those questions are real inconvenient," she says.

"What's that supposed to that mean?" Frances says.

"Nothing. Whatever."

"Honey, listen, I wanted to talk to you about something." From across the lake she hears a jet ski. Some people don't know when to end the party. "Your school counselor called last week."

Emily expels a puff of air through her nose.

"She told me you brought a condom to school," Frances tells her.

"It was a dare." Emily sticks her bare foot into the lake. "That's the truth."

"Are you sure, sweetie?" You need to open these doors slowly, Frances thinks. Rushing headlong into a conversation about a certain boy and where his hands have been is a recipe for shutdown.

"That counselor is a bitch, Mom. She's out to get me."

"I wasn't terribly impressed with her, either. But watch your language."

"She lies. Plus she thinks all girls are boy-crazy."

"Because you can talk to me about sex any time you need to."

"Okay, all right. Just, okay. Gross."

She gives Emily a one-armed hug around the shoulders. It feels good to have broached the subject. "Okay, then," she says. "What about school, otherwise?"

"It's fine," Emily says. She grabs her hair as if to form a ponytail. She's done this since she was a little girl, as a way of occupying her hands. She'll smooth it and form it, work out the bumps, then let it go and start again.

"Classes okay? Teachers?"

"Why are you interested all of a sudden?" Emily's fingers catch on pillow-knots.

"Here," Frances says. "Let me give you a braid." She takes Emily's hair out of her hands and begins to work it into a French braid, as if they're getting ready for a recital or someone's wedding. They face the water, Frances standing behind Emily. Her hair smells of green apple shampoo.

"Can't beat moonlight on a lake," Frances says.

"You aren't even using a comb. It's going to come out crappy," Emily says.

"Somebody you're looking to impress, out here in the woods?" Frances says.

"Why are you always making fun of me?" Emily says. She starts to jerk her head away, but her hair is entwined in Frances's fingers. Reflexively, Frances tightens her grip.

"I'm just teasing, sweetheart," Frances says. "But I'll try to stop doing that if it hurts your feelings." How did this child turn out so touchy? Frances wonders. She begins a mental catalog of her own relatives, searching for someone prickly. Someone from whom Emily might have inherited all this sensitivity.

"Why didn't you get an abortion?" Emily mumbles, softly.

"What? You mean when I was pregnant with you? Emily! Aren't we done with that question?" Frances says. She stops braiding and tugs Emily's hair to the side so she can see her face.

"Ow," Emily says. "Jeez. Never mind."

"I wanted you, that's why," Frances says. There's no reason for her to tell Emily that she nearly went through with the abortion; that she'd cancelled her appointment, thinking her boyfriend might stick around if there was a baby. No reason for Emily to know her mother was as typical and unoriginal and deluded as any other pregnant teenager in the history of pregnant teenagers.

"How did you know you wanted me if you didn't even know who I was?"

"I just knew, Emily." Frances needs to rethink her parenting strategy. She needs to adapt.

On the road the next afternoon Todd says, "I want to call Daddy."

Frances believes in not withholding their father from them, so she hands back her cell phone and tells him to go ahead and call. Also, she wants the guy to be reminded that his sons think about him almost constantly. And that Frances is the kind of mother who goes to the trouble of taking her children on family adventures.

She doesn't remember, until it's too late, that Robbie knows the significance of Memphis. All those alarmists screaming about marijuana and memory loss might actually be on to something. "Mom," says Todd. "Daddy wants to talk to you."

"You've got to be kidding me, Fran," Robbie says. She hears music in the background, and voices.

"Where are you, in a bar?" Frances says into the phone. "At one o'clock in the afternoon?"

Emily unbuckles her seat belt and climbs back to sit with the boys.

"It's an office party," he says. "Someone's birthday. Why do you say things like that when the boys can hear you? Jesus Christ. Tell me you're not going to see Maury. You're not bringing the boys to Memphis to see Maury."

"Oh, we're great," she says, brightly. "They're having a great time." Frances peeks at Emily and notices she's trying to get the boys to play "I Spy." Lately Frances has noticed Emily's worry attaching itself to the boys.

"I swear to God, Fran." Phone reception notwithstanding, Robbie sounds so much like himself, the kind of guy that women smarter than Frances happily take to bed but never marry. When they'd been dating for a month or so, he'd brought her to a spot in the Coronado National Forest where he'd been cultivating a plot of marijuana plants. It had taken them two hours to hike in, stepping carefully to avoid leaving a path. They'd had a picnic at the edge of his plot, the dense buds, backlit by the low sun, looking like multiple furry penises protruding from each stalk. He'd explained to her that they were surrounded by females: that in the world of cannabis, women are the only desirable sex; that the male is mostly leaves and doesn't grow those dense, resinous floral clusters. "A male," he said, "carries genes that influence the quality of his female offspring, but on his own he's worthless. You grow him only to evaluate his potency. If you can use him to pollinate yourself some kick-ass girl plants, you keep him around." He lit a joint. "Then you clone your best girls and away we go." They got carelessly high, lying on a cotton blanket in the shade of his bright green plants. "Yep," he said, after they'd had the kind of slow-motion sex made more intense by the hypersensitivity of their mucous membranes, "the value of the male is defined by the quality of his daughters."

Listening to that voice now on the cell phone, Frances reminds herself that in the end she hated him too much to fuck him no matter how high she was. It had taken her years to discover that his counterculture attitude was nothing more than a cover for a lifestyle supported by credit cards and a refusal to take anything seriously, including their family.

"Just don't do anything stupider than you've already done," Robbie says. "I hope your goddamn barracuda divorce lawyer knows a thing or two about criminal law, because if you get busted, everything's going to hell."

She flips the phone closed. For a brief beat in the visor mirror she and Emily look into each other's eyes.

Whatever happened to the good old-fashioned truck stop diner, Frances wonders. She envisioned root beer floats, milkshakes in metal mixing cups, she and the boys and Emily sitting in a row on chrome barstools. But for dinner they've ended up in a convenience store truck stop that houses a series of miniature fast food franchises. Emily wants a fish sandwich, Robbie a hot dog. These places, Frances is sure, are purposefully designed to split up the American family, and as an added benefit to cause mothers the special kind of anxiety that results from their children scattering in a public place. She follows Todd to a self-serve Slurpee machine and lets him pull the handle, releasing the slush into a plastic Arkansas Razorbacks cup.

They reconvene in a booth constructed of bright orange laminate with sticky brown soda rings on the surface. Robbie chose the spot, making a beeline for a table as close as possible to two Border Patrol agents sucking on tubs of soda, hunched over quantities of fast food. Great, Frances thinks: a new fascination with cops. She sips halfheartedly on a diet Pepsi.

Emily holds out her hand for the car key. She needs her backpack to go to the bathroom.

"What for?" Robbie says, loudly. "You need a tampon?"

"Shut up, butthead," Emily says. Her period started only six months ago, later than all of her friends. Shortly thereafter Robbie pulled a Kotex out of the box in the hall bathroom and ran around the front yard with the pad stuck to his forehead. Frances can't tell whether his age-inappropriate fascination with menstruation is based on scientific curiosity or purely on the joy of infuriating his sister.

Frances and the boys have finished their refreshments by the time Emily emerges from the bathroom. She's walking slowly and has an oddly serious look on her face. Frances begins to scoot out of the booth, to see what's the matter, when Emily opens her backpack and pulls out something wrapped in duct tape. A Ziploc bag. Emily stops five booths away, looking Frances in the eye. The two Border Patrol agents are seated exactly between them. She's openly holding the package of weed, but has positioned the backpack to block it from their view.

"Robbie put ice in my hair!" Todd yells.

Frances meets Emily's gaze. She stands up.

"Mom!" Todd says. "Tell him to quit it!"

"Hush now," Frances says. The boys crane their necks to see what she's looking at.

Emily hasn't moved. "Emily?" Frances says. "Honey?"

One of the Border Patrol agents raises his head.

"What, Mom?" Todd shouts. "What's wrong with Emily?"

Emily stuffs the package into her backpack. She continues to look directly at Frances. Apparently Frances's lectures on the importance of maintaining eye contact have not gone unheeded. On their way back to the car, her knees threaten to buckle.

Emily herds the boys into the van, gets them settled into the farthest seat back, the spot Todd calls the *wayback*. They hook into headphones with a Jackie Chan movie.

In the passenger seat Emily cries, quietly, for twenty miles.

"How did you get to it?" Frances finally says. On the opposite side of the interstate, headlights approach, then race on. All those people inside all those cars, hurtling across the darkened landscape.

"Last night. At the campground," Emily tells her. "I wanted to make sure you weren't going to give away any of my stuff. I just was looking for my stuff, Mom."

"I told you, Emily, I wouldn't give away your things."

"Why should I believe you? You lie to me all the time."

"I do no such thing, Emily. And we're not doing this right now. The boys."

"The boys, right. The boys." But Emily looks back at them.

"I'm warning you, Emily. I swear to God. You have no idea. You think you're such a grown-up. Such an adult. Such the responsible one. Let me tell you. Let me say this."

"Shush, Mom," Emily says.

"Do you know anything at all about credit cards?" Frances says. "Do you know about 19 percent interest? Do you know how much, in dollars and cents, it would cost a single mother of three to pay off twenty thousand dollars? Take a guess. How many pairs of new sneakers is that? How many pounds of hamburger?"

Emily's mouth opens unattractively. Her jaw is being pulled down, Frances thinks, by the dead weight of all that ignorant righteousness.

"Would you at least whisper?" Emily says.

"Take a guess! How about mortgages? What do you know about mortgages?" Frances is now yelling. "What do you know about personal bankruptcy? And while we're at it, how about divorce? What happens, exactly, when the custodial parent is deemed financially insolvent? Any answers yet, missy? Anything else you want to add? Anything you can do better than me here? Maybe you'd like to drive this car? Get us to Memphis?"

It occurs to Frances to check the rearview mirror. The boys have removed their headphones and are peering over the seat in front of them at their crying sister. Two wrinkled brows, two pairs of startled eyes, two furry heads edged in light from the cars on the road behind them.

"It's okay, boys," Emily says. "I'm okay."

"Nothing to see here," Frances says. "Enough gawking."

At ten o'clock, Frances pulls over at a rest stop outside Little Rock. While Emily and the boys are in the bathrooms brushing their teeth she calls Maury. "I can't meet you in friggin' Arkansas, Fran," he says. "Jason has one of his god-awful violin recitals first thing in the morning. If I miss another one Eileen is going to divorce me. You're only two hours away, give or take. Ring the bell when you get here, wake me up. We'll have beds ready for you and the kids. Tomorrow we'll grill some burgers, the kids will go for a swim. Hang tough."

Emily and the boys climb back into their seats and Frances forces the car eastward. Were there a bridge over the interstate right here, a convenient way to turn around, she might have yielded to the urge to head back home. She tells the boys to take out their pillows and lay down. They drape a blanket over the seats and make a fort, which means she can't look at them sleeping. She lets them curl up with seatbelts buckled around their waists and tries not to think about the reasons this is unsafe. Emily reclines the passenger seat and falls asleep, or pretends to. She's such a little girl. Such a small, fatherless thing.

By midnight, pretty much the only vehicles on the road are tractor-trailers. Frances drinks coffee and thinks about life as a long-haul driver, how uncomplicated and free of strings it must be. How quiet.

She takes the first exit after the enormous bridge across the Mississippi into Memphis. Mud Island Park is nearly deserted. She finds a spot under a burned-out streetlight at the far edge of the park. She wants to be close to the water, to watch the current under the bright moon and appreciate its vast wideness. Suddenly she's no longer in a hurry to get to Maury's house. She'll sleep for an hour or so in this quiet van with her tousled children, their mouths open, their bodies having begrudgingly adapted to these makeshift beds. The boys' fort has collapsed; Emily's pillow has fallen to the floor. She is dreaming. Todd stirs, and raises his head. "Are we there?" She shakes her head, puts her finger to her lips, and he's asleep again, too tired to be curious.

Frances slips from the car. She walks down a short path to the edge of the water. The river is flat and slow and wide, entirely as she expected. A barge passes, its lights distant and comforting.

Emily has never been good with life's gray areas. She's a child: children feel most comforted in the presence of clarity about right and wrong.

Had Frances's marriage worked out, it's possible that Robbie's easygoing nature might have had a positive effect on Emily. During the final years, Frances thought the two of them were even starting to develop a mild respect for one other. But she's not Robbie, and she's not about to try parenting her daughter the way Robbie might have done. Tomorrow Frances will take a walk with Emily, maybe take her to lunch, leave the boys with Maury and Eileen. They'll talk. She'll clear everything up.

She smokes a whole joint. She needs to sleep soundly, needs to dull the effect of the coffee and the discomfort of the driver's seat and the heaviness in her gut. In the morning she'll feel fuzzyheaded and drained, but for now she needs the familiar numbness of her own finely cultivated weed. A little smoke helps her, it really does, to put things in perspective, to keep the despair manageable. She stands there for a long time, watching the stillness.

⚬⚬⚬

Emily opens her eyes and watches her mother at the river's edge. She does not need to see the joint to know what's going on. And when the idea to toss her mother's marijuana into the actual Mississippi River comes into Emily's head, there is no chasing it out. Nothing else can be done. She thinks and thinks and thinks about it, and finally she cannot imagine their future unfolding any other way.

After a while, her mother returns to the van and Emily keeps her eyes closed and waits for her to fall very soundly asleep. She waits a long time. For a girl her age, Emily has an unusual capacity for patience.

Lately, at home, when Emily wakes up in the night, she experiences a desire to go to her mother's bedroom and climb into bed with her, like she used to do before the boys were born. The night before they left on this trip, Emily even got so far as her bedside. When her mother's asleep she looks older, and just as impatient as she does when she's awake. Emily didn't, last week, get into bed with her mother, and now she wishes she had.

In the driver's seat her mother sleeps with her head thrown back, looking like nothing could wake her up. Her stale marijuana breath fills the car. The soft click of the keys slipping from the ignition doesn't disturb her. Emily is careful to turn off the dome light before she opens the door.

She moves quietly, looking where she steps to avoid snapping twigs or sending a loose rock skittering. She's a careful girl; she's always been careful, and not very well appreciated.

For the hundredth time that day, she thinks about Miguel. It's nearly ten o'clock back home; he'll be in his room, playing video games. When her mom was at the river's edge, Emily swiped her cell phone from the glove box. When she's done with the duffel bags she'll call Miguel, who will tease her about sneaking off to call him. He says she needs to quit being so good. She should skip doing her homework once in a while, for example. Also she should let him do more than she currently allows. Let him put it in other places; let him do it in different ways. He's seventeen, he's reminded her. He needs to experiment. She's always thought her goodness is the thing about her that keeps him around; that he wouldn't find her so mysterious if she weren't so good, but maybe she's been wrong.

The lock on the cargo carrier opens easily. The two duffel bags are just where she found them last. They aren't really that heavy. She pulls them out and sets them in the dirt. As she's easing the lid shut, she looks in the van's window and there's Todd, awake. He opens his mouth to say something and she puts her finger to her lips. Obediently, he shuts up. She moves quickly to the passenger door and motions him forward. She smiles at him, and raises her eyebrows. He loves adventures. He's really not such a horrible kid, when you get him alone.

She holds the duffel bags in one hand and Todd's elbow in the other, helping him quietly down the path, away from the van. At the water's edge she gives him the daisy duffel bag; he'll be reluctant to throw away anything with soccer balls on it. She tells him it's full of zucchini and carrots. He believes her; he still trusts people. "But it's wasting vegetables!" he says, delighted. He tries to swing it, to get some momentum. "It's heavy," he says, his little-boy forehead wrinkled in seriousness.

"Do this," Emily tells him, and she swings the other duffel around in a full-armed circle, like a crazed softball pitcher. Todd laughs aloud.

In her pocket, the phone rings. Emily slings the duffel bag over her shoulder and fishes the phone out. Miguel wouldn't call her mom's cell phone, would he?

"Frances?" says the voice. It's Robbie. She's supposed to think of him as her stepfather but really he's nothing more than her brothers' dad.

"No, she's asleep," Emily tells him. "It's late here, you know."

"Is it daddy?" Todd says too loudly, forgetting they're on a secret mission. "Let me talk to him!" He drops the daisy duffel in the mud and reaches for Emily's arm, tugging at her shirt.

"Is that one of the boys?" Robbie asks. "What are they doing up? Where are you?"

Todd dances in circles around Emily, trotting like a pony. "Daddy! We're by the river!" he yells.

"We're fine," she tells him, and hands the phone to her brother. "Keep your voice down," she says, and for good measure knits her eyebrows.

Lately Emily has begun to understand the tricky nature of mistruth, of roundabout deception. In real life people don't lie to you straight up. Miguel doesn't lie to her, not exactly. It's up to her to discover things. She has a gift for recognizing a half-truth. Last Friday Emily was alone with him on the couch in her basement and he swore he didn't mean to put it all the way in, not without the condom she'd laid on the table—and when they happen, these halfway lies, when she confronts him, he smiles at her, confesses, and is chastened, genuinely. She holds the power then: she's the one who decides whether he's forgiven. But what if she got pregnant? Would she end up with more power, or less?

Todd chatters into the phone. The kid doesn't get enough time with his dad. Emily sits on a rock, her back to her brother, and opens the duffel bag. She pulls out one of the bundles, smells it, turns it over in her hands. She thinks about the time and energy her mother put into creating this tidy parcel of drugs, and examines the package, how neatly and carefully it's been assembled. She did a nice job, Emily thinks, and then wonders why this is surprising. She zips it back inside the bag.

"Here," her brother says, handing her the phone. He canters a few steps away, bends to pick up a stick, and begins poking at a patch of mud illuminated by moonlight.

"Emily?" his father says. "What's going on there? Todd says your mom and Robbie are asleep in the van? And you guys are near a river somewhere?"

"The Mississippi," she tells him.

"Is everything all right?"

"Sure," she says. The bag of drugs on her lap weighs, she guesses, a little bit more than a sack of potatoes.

"Are you crying? Sweetie?"

Emily tries to calm her breath. "She's such a liar," she finally says. Juxtaposed against all those years of thinking of this guy as an interloper between her and her mother, and the despair, then resignation, she lived through after the arrival of one baby and then a second, Emily's disloyalty is both liberating and horrible.

Robbie sounds now like he's holding his breath. "What do you mean?"

"You know what I mean. The pot is what."

"Oh, Emmy. Damn." She heard the impatience in his voice.

"How much is all of this worth?" she asks.

"Honey, this isn't appropriate. Why don't you wake up your mom? I'd like to talk to her."

"I'm sitting here with two duffel bags full of marijuana," Emily whispers. She glances over her shoulder. Todd is still occupied with his mud project. "Looks like each one has six packages in it, and each package is about the size of a brick. Like the red bricks on our back patio, only not so heavy. Just tell me. How much?"

He coughs, clears his throat. "Emily, listen to me. Put your mom on the phone."

"I'm about to throw it all in the river," she says.

"About twenty thousand dollars," he says. "Maybe twenty-five."

Emily inhales, but quietly. "Listen," Robbie tells her. "You know your mother. Sometimes her judgment . . . well. She loves you, you know that, right? But she doesn't think things through. She goes headlong, consequences be damned. Responsibility isn't her strength."

"Like it's yours," Emily says.

"Okay, now—"

She cranes her neck to check on Todd, who is behind her, gripping the daisy duffel at arm's length, whipping it in a circle parallel to the ground, his little body the fulcrum of a centrifugal spin. He stops, staggers, gives her a dizzy grin. "Put that down," she tells him. "Don't touch it." He grimaces at her and returns to his mud and stick.

The muddy river glows orange in the Memphis night. "You people think I don't know anything," she says into the phone. "Mom thinks I have no idea. I can read, you know. I understand things."

"Would you wake up your mother, Emily? Would you please just put her on the phone?"

"I know how to balance a checkbook, for example," she tells him. She also knows how much money he sends them and when it's not enough and when it's late and what happens when her mother can't make a deposit. She taught herself how go online and examine the bank accounts and credit card statements. After school, before her mother gets home from work, Emily logs in using the password she created and watches in dismay and sometimes panic as interest compounds and checks bounce and the late fees pile up. Last month she sent MasterCard two hundred dollars from her own savings. She went to the post office and converted her baby-sitting cash into a money order. Her mother didn't even notice.

"I'm not all that awful, you know," he tells her.

"I didn't realize we were talking about you," Emily says.

Robbie sighs into the phone, an irritating burst of static. Emily wonders if he's a little bit high right now. Wouldn't a sober person realize it's the middle of the night in Memphis and wait until morning to call? "Are you all right?" he says. "Have you spoken to your mother about this?"

"We've been talking plenty." But last night at the lake in Oklahoma, when Emily tried to confess she's been having sex with Miguel, when she tried to bring up the subject, her mother purposefully misunderstood. What's a kid supposed to think when she asks her mother, *What would happen if I got an abortion?* and the woman pretends she heard a whole other sentence? Is a kid supposed to believe the weed is to blame?

Behind her, up the path, Emily hears the car door slam shut. At the same instant there is a splash in the river. She turns to see Todd jumping gleefully on the shore. "What a pitch!" he yells, and cups his hands over his mouth, exhaling noisily to create the sound of cheering crowds. "Ladies and gennelmen! The kid does it again!"

"Todd?" Emily's mother calls. "Emily? What was that?" She runs down the path, toward the water. Robbie emerges from the van, barefoot, following gingerly behind her.

A pocket of air inflates the round end of the duffel Todd has just thrown; it looks like a pink-daisy lily pad bobbing lazily downriver. He must have had real momentum behind his fling to have gotten it so far.

Emily's mom stands helplessly at the water's edge, her hands on the top of her head. "Oh no, no, no," she says. She crouches in the mud. The resignation on her face, Emily notices for the first time, is that of a person for whom despair is part of the everyday. "Shit," she whispers.

Todd claps his hands over his ears.

Emily drops the phone, kicks off her sandals, and steps firmly into the river, wet silt slimy between her toes, the cold a surprise. She flops into the water belly first, and in five certain strokes downstream catches the bag in her fingertips just as it loses the last of its air and slips under the surface.

When Emily turns toward the shore, eyes bleary with the Mississippi, her mother's moonlit face holds a curious mixture of admiration and terror. Which seems just about right.

the nigerian princes

o silence their noise about giving them grandchildren, I've let my parents believe that my best friend Ramón is my lover. They're too old to embrace homosexuality but know better than to admit that. They're in their seventies, and I'm their only child.

Truth is, I can't keep a girlfriend. Louise looks at me now as if I'm the copy machine repair guy. Right through me. I'm sad most of the time, but let's face it; everyone is sad. Everyone except Ramón. He says that Louise is invested in the story of herself and that I shouldn't give up on her. He told me he saw her on the roof of our office building at lunch today, her chin tilted toward the sun as if her own life were too tragic for this world.

Louise: her hands, her lips, the curve of her brow. I used to think her face would be with me always. I would have been there for the aging of those hands, the wrinkle of that forehead. I imagine her an old woman, thin-skinned, thin-haired, rheumy-eyed and beautiful in an Irish cardigan on the beach in wintertime. The gulls, the pipers, the wind bringing blood to her cheeks. Me an old man, grateful and quiet and finally responsible.

The Nigerian Princes were our hobby, Louise and me. Those assholes. Stealing money from old ladies and crazy people. They offended us. You'd have to be either sadly naïve or mentally ill to get caught in their scam. You'd have to live outside the reach of human interaction, which on top of everything else would mean you're also lonely. This is the demographic those assholes are after. The unfairness of it killed me.

I can't keep a girlfriend and I can't find a wife. I've been trying, Ramón will attest to it. With Louise I fucked it up again. I fucked it up good.

My mother is a displacement artist. She puts things where they don't belong. When I was a kid, arts councils kept giving her grants. Her work is a statement on consumption, and identity, and place. I would come home from third grade and find one of her utilitarian brassieres in the refrigerator, a cluster of red grapes cradled in each cup. The family weed whacker, encrusted with Bermuda, mounted inside a gilt frame on the dining room wall. In the supermarket I'd wander away from her, bored, and among the comic books I'd come upon a dozen key limes displayed in an open egg carton. A tidy row of Idaho russet potatoes set atop stacks of spiral-bound notebooks.

My father is a literature professor, retired. Emeritus. Charles Dickens was the genius at the center of my childhood. If Dickens were alive and in need of a baggage handler or someone to suck his dick, my dad would have been the man for the job.

"Fehgele for Dickens, your husband," Ramón told my mother authoritatively last year at the Seder table. The old man had just delivered to us a fresh theory refuting the accusations of anti-Semitism in *Oliver Twist*. Ramón loves my mom, idiot that he is. Also he'll eat anything, including her horrendous cooking. He's freakishly accomplished at dinner conversation, so his presence at holiday meals works out for everyone.

My mother guffawed lovingly at Ramón. Wiped tears of laughter with her palsied arthritic hand. Dad grinned amiably through his deafness.

Ramón is neither gay nor Jewish.

Incoming interoffice email. From Louise. *Forgiveness?* It says. *Forgiveness is for pussies.*

My mother thinks Louise is my fag hag. This according to Ramón, in whom she confides. Ramón thinks Mom's a scream. But consider the context: Ramón was raised by human traffickers. He spent much of his childhood in the back of unmarked vans stinky with the sweat of individuals scared shitless. He'd have been thrilled to find an unwashed carrot and a can of sardines in his lunchbox, as I did in seventh grade, four days in a row.

In the break room at work, Ramón eyes a bowl of chocolate kisses somebody brought for Valentine's Day. The office is lousy with glitter and sugar. Ramón needs to lose about eighty pounds.

"She still loves you, dude," he says. "Don't be intimidated by the evil eye."

I told him about the email she sent this morning.

"Yeah, well," he says. "The woman's got to vent. Venting is what you want. Believe me."

"You don't know shit," I tell him.

"Not true," he says, succumbing to the Hershey's. "I do know shit. Shit I learned from you, in fact. For example, I know that Nigerian Princes can be real assholes."

"Fuck you, Ramón." I fish around for a dark chocolate kiss. "And keep your voice down, for chrissake."

Harassing the Nigerian Princes was something Louise and I could do together. We knew that couples tend to split up when they don't have common interests, like surfing, or scrapbooking, or smoking weed. Until we started fucking with the Nigerian Princes, Louise and I were heading down that road. She had her bitter feminist book group and her beer-drinking rock climbers and I had my Neanderthal white guy football Sundays and my language poetry workshop. The Nigerian Princes brought us back to one another.

Louise has a wicked dark imagination and a pitch-perfect understanding of character development. Her knack for detail is astonishing. *Meet me at Lufthansa luggage carousel number five in Oslo,* she'd email a Nigerian Prince. *I'll be wearing a desert camouflage maxi skirt and a black pageboy wig. Africans make me anxious, so be sure to approach slowly and leave any tribal accoutrements (masks and spears and whatnot) back in your village. I'll get my nephew to strap the cash to my upper thigh and will probably need your help retrieving it, considering my bulk prevents me from accessing certain parts of my body, lol.*

Louise would cackle as she typed. Lying on her stomach on the bed, laptop before her. This would make me hard as a rock. I'd lift her skirt and pull her up by the hips and slip inside her. Bent over the keyboard she'd cackle and type, type and cackle and moan.

Louise and I weren't alone in our preoccupation with Nigerian Prince harassment. There are clubs, websites, support groups. It's not as if we were the only people to pursue the hobby on company time, either: a guy from Massachusetts named Leon runs a listserv for counterscammers out of his cubicle at Google. "Difference is, he's not an ignorant asshole," pointed out Louise, the night we came home from work, stunned and freaked out at the news that the company's mainframe had been hacked and the credit card numbers of twenty thousand customers stolen, and by the likelihood that our taunting of the Nigerian Princes was responsible.

Incoming interoffice email. From Jerry, my boss. *Your external audit team interview scheduled for next Tuesday.*

It's only a matter of time before they figure out it was us. Or Louise, technically. Because I was the one who told her my computer was offline when it actually wasn't, that night months ago when she and I took a graveyard shift for the overtime pay, working all night in jeans and T-shirts, in a maze of empty cubicles. First we fucked in my office chair, then in hers, then in our department manager's. Then we decided to fuck with the Nigerians for a little while. And I knew, somewhere in a dark corner of my idiot reptilian brain, that sending emails to Nigeria from your desktop was the sort of thing that gets you fired. It was me who told her it would be fine to use her computer, no way they'd find out, no way they'd even care. I told her it would all be okay.

And then, in my despair, I admitted to her what I'd done. At which point she started, rightfully, to hate me. Louise has a kid named Janie, a six year old with blue eyes and red curly hair and fucking cerebral palsy. Preexisting conditions up the yin-yang, dependent on company healthcare for her meds, her wheelchair, her oxygen tank, her physical therapists, her specialists, her daycare, her survival. Louise's anger at me is primal.

"Listen," Ramón says. "Your mom has a plan."

"For what?"

"To rescue your job, you idiot."

Telling my mother about my professional fiascos is precisely the sort of thing you could expect from Ramón. I smack him upside the head with the flat of my palm.

"Ow," he says. "Okay, ow."

"You're a lousy gay lover, you know it?" I tell him.

"I do it because I care," he lisps, rubbing his temple. His suit jacket is dusted with flakes of dandruff. He's just a customer service rep like me.

There's no need for the suit, but that's Ramón for you. "Your mom says we should hack into the mainframe ourselves, erase your email trail."

"This was my mother's idea?" I say. "To hack into the mainframe?"

"OK, we came up with the plan together." Ramón opens the fridge, releasing the garbagey smell of leftover lunches into the break room. "She's willing to finance the operation, though."

"I need you to quit hanging out with my mom."

"We have a relationship that exists independently of you," he tells me.

Louise comes into the break room, wearing that blouse I bought her for Hanukah last year, the one that makes her tits look so fabulous. She sees me in my stained khakis and sleep-deprived face. "Your fly is down, dickwad," she says.

"Hey, Louise," Ramón says, sotto voce. "Meet me on the roof at lunch. We've got a plan for saving your job."

Louise fixes Ramón with one of her testicle-withering stares. "Who does?" she whispers. "You and dickwad here?"

I hold my hands palm-forward in innocence. "This has nothing to do with me."

"God forbid you have a plan," Louise says.

Louise doesn't let me help her with Janie. She's a single mom, working full time, with a kid in a wheelchair. We've been living together for a year and I've never picked up Janie, not even to help her out of her chair. Louise won't even let me sweep up the Cheerios Janie knocks over with that hand of hers, shrunken and twisted as it is, her soft fleshy claw. Underneath all that piteous frustration about her body, Janie's a kid with a good heart and a sweet smile. I don't know how Louise manages not to be crying all the time.

Incoming extraoffice email. From Her Highness Mrs. Wife of His Highness Mgote: *You are very stupid, this is not a scam but a pay back, are u cognizant about what the white man came to do to my grandfathers. You do not know what they stole from Nigerian kingdom. This is justice time.*

The external auditor is skinny, with bad teeth and glasses all wrong for his face. He asks me questions and I answer them with lies. No, I have never used my corporate email account to send personal messages. Except for sometimes, I say, for verisimilitude, to my mother. I shrug, and tell the guy that Mom doesn't understand professional boundaries.

On my way back to my cubicle Ramón pulls me into the men's room. "So?" he says. "How'd it go?"

"I'm golden," I tell him. "We bonded over impossible mothers."

"Don't get cocky. These guys are fucking animals, believe me. And speaking of mothers. Dinner at Mom's tonight. Seven o'clock."

"Whose Mom?" I say.

"Yours, idiot. Mine is dead, remember? Who's the lousy boyfriend now?"

At the front door to her house that evening, my mother throws her arms around Ramón's neck. "My dear!" she cries. Over his shoulder, she shows me a steely eyeball. We sit at the table. She's prepared a supper of kalamata olives, dried figs, and peanut butter on crackers. And champagne.

"I know a guy," she screeches, so my father can hear. "He knows all about computers. He'll break into your office and wipe out the evidence. I asked him and he said yes."

The peanut butter is the all-natural kind, ineptly stirred. It's thin and oily and dripping off my cracker. "It's not that easy, Mom," I say.

"Your mother is afraid for the little crippled girl," my father yells. "Damn shame! Corporate healthcare is a crock of shit!"

"Disabled, Dad. She has a disability," I articulate.

"All so you could amuse yourself," my mother says. "Nigerians, dear? Why Nigerians? Could you not accomplish this . . ." she looks helplessly at Ramón.

"Scam baiting," he supplies.

". . . on your own time? Instead you indulge your hobby at work? Did you not realize you were playing with that little girl's *life*?"

Ramón picks gamely at his olives and figs. "Go easy on him, Irene," he murmurs.

"Interesting that you care so much, mother," I say. "Given your feelings about Louise."

My mother flaps her hands in dismissal. "I don't give a shit about that woman, are we clear? But the little girl, a little girl in a wheelchair with no health insurance, it's a nightmare. I feel responsible!"

"Louise's computer was confiscated today," I say.

"What?" my father yells.

"It's too late, Dad," I shout back. "The auditors took her computer. They'll analyze the keystrokes or whatever they do. They'll find a record of the emails to Nigeria. We're too late, Dad! We're too late."

As I speak, my father's eyes are bouncing frantically between Ramón and me. "You're not gay?" he says. He looks at my mother in alarm. "Isn't that what he said, dear? The boy's not gay!"

"He said we're too late!" My mother cries, leaping from her seat. "We're too late!" She scampers to his chair and stands behind him, clamping his shoulders in a dramatic little embrace.

"And for the record, people, I'm not gay," I say.

My mother releases my father's shoulders. "Ramón? Is this true?"

Ramón reaches for the back of her neck, holds it affectionately. "He's in love with Louise, sweetie," he admits. "Not me."

"What?" my father says. "What the hell did he just say?"

"He's not gay," my mother enunciates, bending to his ear. "That awful woman is the girlfriend."

"And the handicapped girl?" my father asks.

And here goes the whir of Ramón's genius idiot brain. "Your grandchild!" he tells them.

A fair trade. A lie for a lie. Ramón is the best friend I've ever had.

Incoming extraoffice email from Her Highness Mrs. Wife of His Highness Mgote: *Africa is the birthplace of humanity you are idiot American. Return all the things you steal from our ancestors. We will hit you guys until you stop making child slavery and weapons of mass destruction.*

But the security breach turns out to have originated from a couple of teenage identity thieves in Coeur d'Alene, Idaho. When the companywide email arrives announcing the discovery, I stand up in my cubicle and wait with a hopeful grin for Louise's head to appear over her partition. I fucked it up so badly, she has no reason to forgive me.

On her face is an oceanic event of happiness, an underground earthquake of relief, a maternal tide. Someday we'll end up on our beach, Louise and me, ancient versions of ourselves tottering through the loose sand, she thinking it's her arm keeping me upright and me thinking it's mine around her. We will have lived a long life of tribulation and pain and humor and unremarkable joy. The Nigerian Princes will have become grandparent lore. I can nearly feel her bones through the linen tunic she'll be wearing, through her thin elderly skin, through the toneless muscles. In all my long life I will never have desired a woman like I do this one.

Later the security team calls Louise into their office to inform her that in the course of their investigation they found the Nigerian Prince emails. They give her two weeks' severance pay.

In my arms that night she sobs. She feels foolish, it was her fault as much as mine, she says. She's a mother, she's supposed to be responsible, she cannot play loose with her crappy job. The weight of Janie's condition threatens to crack the bedframe. To pull us, mattress and all, through the floor to the apartment below. We're heavy, is what I'm saying. A dump-truck of river rock, a thousand iron safes. But she's taken me back, she's forgiven me, and I will never, ever, fuck up again. I pull her on top of me to take her weight, to cushion her landing.

In the morning, the UPS guy delivers a state-of-the-art pediatric wheelchair. With a pink and purple frame and sparkly ribbons woven between the spokes. I come out of the shower to find Louise frowning over the thing, which is parked in the living room like a Christmas bicycle. Janie is wild-eyed and clapping.

"What the fuck is going on?" Louise asks me. She waves the packing slip. "Your mother did this?"

"It's Ramón's fault."

"That bitch. These things cost five grand." She stabs at the keypad on her cell phone. "Ramón!" she says when he picks up. "What have you done?"

Louise goes silent, eyes wide and tearing as she locks my gaze, and I know he's telling her about the trust fund my parents started for Janie and the health insurance policy they spent a fortune on, and he's delivering the news in the way I couldn't, in just exactly the right language. Goddamn Ramón always comes out smelling like a lemon cupcake.

The wheelchair is lightweight, half the width of the behemoth Janie has so much trouble navigating, plus the kid loves it. She's screeching to be freed from her old chair, screeching for Louise to hang up the phone.

I lift Janie. She's wobbly-headed and too light for her age. Louise gasps a little and holds three fingers against her lips. Gently I put Janie down, settling her into her new ride.

i love bob

illary's father was Bob Barker. From the TV game show. But he didn't know this, so at the end of her sophomore year at Coconino Community College she drove from Flagstaff to Los Angeles to tell him in person. She'd stay for the month of June, long enough to execute her plan.

With tips from her job waiting tables at Denny's, she rented a studio apartment in a stick-and-stucco complex in Van Nuys with walls of cardboard and a swimming pool that sparkled.

Hillary's mother left a voice mail message. "Why did you go all the way to California?" she yelled. "It's pointless, I told you! He's an asshole!" Her mother had been Miss Orange County, 1985. Her career strategy involved walking Bob Barker's dogs four mornings a week and then screwing him afterward. By twenty, she was pregnant and forced to withdraw from the Miss California pageant.

Bob Barker is eighty-two and still hosting the show. Hillary was the same age her mother was when she got pregnant. She cannot imagine sleeping with someone forty years older. If it weren't for ruining her body giving birth to Hillary, her mother might have made it all the way to Miss America.

To escape the dirty mini-blinds in her apartment and the squalling infant next door, Hillary walked over to a pet store at the neighboring strip mall. The puppies slept, ears twitching at the toddler whacking his palms against the glass. She peered at the tropical fish. Three for ten dollars. She considered how long they'd survive in a bowl on her kitchen countertop. She examined the hamsters, which were housed in a large open pen, the fence up to her hip. A little boy poked his fingers through a hole in the mesh. The kid's mother gazed wearily at a bedraggled macaw. A sign on the pen warned customers not to touch the hamsters. A hamster approached the boy's pink finger, sniffed it, and took a nibble. The boy screeched, the mother reacted, and an employee mentioned Sesame Street Band-Aids in the back office, sauntering off to fetch one.

The mother kissed the child's unbroken skin, frowned tenderly into his wet eyes, winked at Hillary. She turned her back to them; functional parenting made her squeamish.

A girl about Hillary's age came into the store. Or was it a boy? This person was skinny, stringy-haired, wearing an oversized army jacket and sparkly blue eyeshadow. He, or she, stooped over the hamster cage as if to pick one up. A chocolate brown hamster poked its head from the sleeve of the army jacket, sniffed the air, and scurried into the pen with the others. The boy-girl looked up and met Hillary's eye. Another hamster, an identical twin, appeared from the same sleeve and jumped nimbly into the cage. They blended into the crowd.

"Hey," the person said, in a voice that was reedy, multitonal, ambisexual.

Hillary tried for a complicit smile.

The employee came back. Bandages, encouragements. This little boy was going to end up with a balloon.

The hamster person shrugged. Olive skin, brown eyes, long lashes. A thin silver nose ring. One wrist bore something tattooed in Chinese." You have no idea how hard it is to unload a hamster."

"I'm beginning to understand," Hillary said. There: an adam's apple. And a boylike toss of the head to shake the hair from his eyes.

"My father said he'd toss them off the Santa Monica pier."

His name was Alex. In the backseat of his Hyundai were six hamster cages, stacked two high. Each cage held four hamsters. The shit from the hamsters on top dropped to the hamsters below. Despite the cracked upholstery and the blotchy paint, Alex's car wasn't a bad ride. The hamsters seemed to be enjoying themselves. The windows were down, and their fur ruffled in the breeze. Fresh-smelling wood shavings lined the bottom cages and blew around the interior of the car. Alex pulled a baggie of romaine lettuce from his pocket and gave it to Hillary to feed the hamsters. Their little jaws chewed furiously. How intense they were, she thought: how focused.

They were on some freeway or another. His hair, and Hillary's, was everywhere. "If you catch them fucking, reach in and pull them apart," he yelled over the wind.

"The boys and girls are together?"

"Yeah, well." Alex said. He rummaged on the dashboard, found a pack of cigarettes and a map. They were doing seventy, but traffic in the left lane still passed them.

"Where are we?" Alex said.

Hillary frowned at the map.

"Look for Interstate Five!" Alex said. "Approaching Glendale!"

Hillary visualized their little white economy vehicle careening toward the Elmgrove Street exit. A cross in purple ballpoint marked the corner of

Crystal and Gatewood. She felt, suddenly, competent. She understood she could rely on her sense of direction, her capacity for leadership, her ability to get them with speed and efficiency from the first cross to the next, to the next, to the next. The hamsters squeaked and scratched. She smoked Alex's cigarettes. The day rolled on, the city warm. Alex's stereo blared bouncy tunes sung by women with guitars. Hillary rested her bare feet on the dashboard and thought kind thoughts about Bob Barker.

They talked about working crappy jobs, about caging pets, about road trips. They saved eighteen hamsters from a saltwater death. They drank diet sodas.

When they stopped to pee at a Texaco, Alex followed her into the women's room. From the stall next to hers she heard him raise the seat. She crouched to look under the partition and there were his boots, facing the toilet. Washing their hands afterward, he grinned at her conspiratorially in the mirror. As girly as he was, he didn't seem gay.

Hillary returned her mother's phone call.

"I'm coming there," her mother said. "I've decided. I'm coming there to spend the summer with my darling kid."

"You'd hate it here," Hillary told her.

"All right, I hear you," her mother said. "Loud and clear! I'll stay home! I'll sit here alone and worry about you getting creamed on some interstate. Running out of food. Getting attacked by a homeless person! You don't want your crazy old mother around!"

Hillary listened for a while longer. Her mother was a practiced alcoholic, her codependencies honed over decades of rehab. It was important not to hang up before she was done talking. Hillary held the phone to her ear and let the words float inside, where they added to the accumulation. As a kid she'd follow her mother into the studio to watch her hands bring another graceful, sad vase into being, coaxing a shape from a lump of wet clay. Over time, her plump vases evolved into spheres, the openings becoming tinier and tinier: the circumference of a pinky. And then there were no openings at all, just globes. Her potter's wheel spun, balancing one wet delicate ball after another. Hillary's task as little girl was to blow a wish to Ptah, the Egyptian god of artisans, when her mother sealed a new top hole with her slurry-slick fingers.

"Ptah," her mother would whisper in a long exhale of wine-spiked breath as Hillary pursed her lips and exhaled into the opening. "Pta-aaaahh." A prayer against wobble. Her mother would seal up the spheres, fire them into ceramic, glaze them in muted greens and grays and sell them to galleries in Miami, Tokyo, Montreal, Brussels.

But inside her mother's fragile spheres, Hillary knew, the air was stinking and gassy. Some day, they would crack under the building pressure of the wine breath and Hillary's pitiful little girl hopes. It might take years, but eventually they would burst, hurling brilliant ceramic shrapnel across living rooms all over the world.

Hillary told Alex about Bob Barker. That evening they rented *Price is Right* episodes from a specialty video store on Sunset Boulevard, a handful from each decade, and watched them late into the night. She sat close to her tiny television and studied Bob Barker's face. Bob Barker *liked* his contestants. This was a man who enjoyed his job. In a show from the nineties, a young woman in a University of Alaska sweatshirt agonized over an array of products, displayed against an orange backdrop. A vacuum cleaner, a trail bike, a Whirlpool side-by-side refrigerator. Bob Barker was so patient with her. This was a man who appreciated humanity.

Contestants were desperate to get onstage, to get close to him. Entire families jumped around in matching T-shirts of pink, lime green, neon yellow, bearing messages of admiration for Bob Barker.

"You've got to let go of your dignity," Alex observed, frowning. "That's how you get picked."

Yes. But Bob made the letting go look benign, even beneficial. Hillary tried to imagine coming to work every day and seeing all those love notes written across the chests of strangers. If she were Bob Barker she would never grow tired of it.

When she made it onstage, Hillary would tell him she was his daughter. She wasn't kidding herself about this plan being wildly unrealistic; she knew there must be better ways to get to him. But this was family. She needed to be there, to see him right up close, no intermediaries. She needed to see his face when he found out.

Onscreen, one of Barker's Beauties caressed an avocado-green electric range. Touching and not touching, the model's manicured hand brushed the appliance, teased, withdrew. A redhead in a micro-miniskirt rode the waves of a king-sized waterbed, arching her eyebrows playfully. Bob had a paternal presence, the way he pretended all that cleavage wasn't really there, those bare thighs weren't bare at all. He never looked directly at the women. He got you to believe he had nothing to do with the decision to display all that flesh.

When Hillary arrived home from the Laundromat the next afternoon, she found her mother asleep on the concrete outside the front door of her apartment. She lay on a comforter from Hillary's old bedroom, her head on her suitcase, legs curled awkwardly around her cosmetics case. She woke as Hillary stepped over her to get inside.

"Sweetie!" she said. "I'm here!"

They went to dinner at the Olive Garden adjoining the mall a block from Hillary's apartment complex, where her mother ate iceberg salad and breadsticks and consumed a full carafe of red wine.

"Do you have a girlfriend yet?" she demanded. "What's the problem there, sweetheart? Are you being nice enough?"

Walking home, she grasped Hillary's arm for balance, surfacing memories of high school. The thing about having a drunk for a mother was that in order to survive, you needed to freeze yourself inside a block of ice.

Her mother landed on the bed. Hillary slept on the floor, atop a grouping of loveseat cushions and throw pillows. In the morning, the familiar stink seeped from her mother's pores and hung in the apartment's airspace. Hillary went through her mother's suitcase. She emptied a flask and a bottle into the kitchen sink. *Keep it Simple*, Hillary thought. *Let Go Let God.* Did her emptying ritual complement or contradict the principle of detachment? If only the Al-Anon meetings at school hadn't been so packed with Jesus freaks she might have stuck with it, to learn coping strategies. Instead she'd invented one of her own, visualizing a smooth ceramic globe embedded in her chest, sealed to contain the odiferous pressure of her childhood.

For her first attempt to see Bob Barker, Hillary arrived in line at the studio before the sun came up. But in the pre-show interview, she competed poorly with the mania of the regular fans. As they waited in the hallway for their turn with the producer, a woman whose T-shirt read KISS ME BOB jumped in place, giggling with anxiety. When it was Hillary's turn to impress, she said, "The *Price is Right* is a great American institution and I want to be a part of history!!" But her cadence was off, and so her attempt at fanaticism emerged belated and sad.

In the audience, Hillary was placed in the second to last row, in a seat partially obstructed by a television monitor. She wasn't called to Come on Down. But it was okay: CBS had scheduled seventeen more tapings in the month of June. Next time she'd invest in a custom T-shirt. BOB'S YOUR UNCLE, maybe. He was old enough to know what it meant.

Bob Barker looked good, he really did, for such an ancient man. His presence made Hillary a little queasy. She put her head between her knees for a minute or two, which helped. She took extensive notes and learned a few things, for example: a single month's supply of Women's Rogaine retailed for $24.99, yet a scünci faux ponytail could be had for only $14.21. The box of two dozen Pampers Feel 'n Learn Advanced Trainers diapers for toddlers was $20.49, yet a thirty-count package of Depends Easy Fit disposable undergarments with Velcro was only $13.99. It cost less to diaper your parents than your kids.

A contestant climbed the Plinko steps and dropped her oversized poker chip into a slot at the top. Bob narrated its progress to the bottom, urging it dramatically with his free hand toward the ten-thousand-dollar niche. When the chip failed to deliver big money, everyone could see his sorrow was sincere. Hillary had once read an article about Mr. Rogers that said he wasn't a television persona at all; his character on the show was his character in real life. Bob Barker too was the real deal. During the commercial breaks, he refrained from ridiculing, even with the slightest of facial expressions, the women in their ill-fitting clothes, the maniacal, screaming audience. He treated every last wingnut as though she were his best friend's mother.

But his makeup, even from Hillary's distance, was alarming in its depth and orangeness. Hillary could see herself in his dressing room, backstage, watching him remove the pancake from his cheeks with cotton balls and cold cream, chuckling with him over the harmless fun of it all.

That afternoon, Hillary and Alex drove around the interstates some more. Between hamster stops, Alex removed his army jacket. Over his skinny jeans and spit-shiny army surplus boots he wore the white billowy blouse of a medieval gentleman. The tassels on the collar were left undone, revealing another Chinese tattoo positioned above a tuft of chest hair. The low sun silhouetted his steering arm through the translucent fabric, revealing a wiry, muscled bicep.

Hillary followed Alex into stores all over the city, distracting employees while Alex birthed hamsters through his sleeves. She was sorry when the last pair was deposited.

They stopped at a Texaco in Encino. Alex paid for the gas with seven dollars and thirty cents in wadded dollar bills from his pocket and a number of coins he'd pried off the floor of the Hyundai. He wouldn't let Hillary pitch in. Which was good, given there were only four dollars in Hillary's purse.

Alex was impressed that Hillary had her own place.

"It's just a studio," Hillary said.

"Still," Alex said. "I want to be gone from my father's house so bad, you can't believe." He held the pump in both hands and shook out the last drop of gasoline.

"But they never really leave you alone," she pointed out.

"Let's eat," Alex said. "I'll make my specialty. Cheap food. Dinner for two, three dollars and fifty cents. Is there a kitchen in this palace you live in?"

Hillary's mother wouldn't be at the apartment: it was happy hour. "Sure," Hillary said. "Also, I own a pan."

At Safeway they bought a pint of milk, a box of Kraft Macaroni & Cheese, and a brick of frozen peas. But when they arrived at the apartment, Hillary's mother was indeed there, asleep, her legs hanging over the end of the loveseat. The place was dim, the odor was present. Why was she surprised? "Crap," Hillary said. She opened the windows in the living room. Light and breeze entered the space. Hillary's mother remained motionless.

"Is she all right?" Alex asked.

They stood over her. The stocking on her left leg had a wide, webby run from ankle to thigh, fully visible given that her mother's legs were sprawled apart. She'd put on weight. The quilt had fallen to the floor. White residue was crusted at the edges of her mouth. "She's kind of a mess," Hillary said.

Alex leaned over Hillary's mom and picked up her hand, turned it over. Her mother didn't stir. "Her lifeline is long," Alex said. "You're in for a ride."

They stood over her like a couple of social workers. "Been on it a while now," Hillary said.

"Unbelievable," Alex said. "How people like us end up finding each other." Alex shook the quilt and draped it over the body of Hillary's mother. They crossed the room to the kitchen, boiled the water, cooked the macaroni, tossed in the peas. Hillary was unaccountably happy to be standing over the stove, touching shoulders with another human being. The orange cheese powder glowed under the fluorescent light. Alex stirred, added the milk. They stared into the pot.

"It's kind of disgusting," Hillary said.

From the loveseat, Hillary's mother grunted in her sleep. Her purse was on the coffee table. Hillary opened it, took her credit card. "Let's eat out," she said.

She left a note: *Dinner's on the stove. Back later.*

They ate sushi and drank miso soup and shared a big silver can of Asahi and talked about Hillary's mother. Alex chewed quickly, closing his eyes to signal a tasty bite. His eye shadow sparkled under the low lamp at their table.

"She's pitiful," Hillary told him. "Imagine. Would you throw yourself at an old man, just to get him to notice you?"

"I'm glad she did," Alex said, meeting her eye.

Hillary poked at her blob of wasabi. "My birth situation is disgusting."

Alex ran his chopstick down her forearm, painting a trail of soy sauce. "Disgusting is in the eye of the beholder," he said.

She raised her arm to her mouth and tongued it clean. His eyes followed her mouth. This would have been the right moment to tell him she wasn't into boys. Except that maybe she was. So she shared her strategy for seeing Bob Barker the next day.

"Solid plan," he said.

"It's stupid. Thanks for not saying so."

"*Au contraire*," he deadpanned. "So what happens when you get onstage?"

Hillary ran her fingers around the rim of the beer can, wishing it weren't empty. The sushi chef's fingerprints were embedded in the lump of wasabi squatting on their plate. Finally she raised her eyes to his face and allowed him to see her confusion.

"My father," Alex said, "is a shit. Can't keep a job, can't say anything real. Afraid of himself, afraid of me, afraid of his own fucking life." Alex snorted, tapped the beer can. Looked for the waitress.

Hillary's gut pinged and ticked, as if the brilliant glaze on the ceramic globe lodged there were sprouting a web of fine crackling threads. She palmed her solar plexus.

"You ok?" Alex said.

"When I was little I had irritable bowel syndrome. Unusual for a kid. Stress related, the doctor said. My mother laughed at him, said what the hell would I have to be stressed out over."

"But he was right," Alex said.

"Actually it turned out to be a tapeworm."

Laughing, he grabbed her hand. He brought her knuckles to his lips and kissed them in dramatic appreciation. She jerked her hand from his mouth reflexively, but he held on and kept holding, teasingly, his breath on her hand as she pulled and pulled, until he saw the change in her eyes and let go.

She told him about the globe. About her mother's fingers sealing it up, about her own little girl breath inside fermenting into toxins, about how the pressure was threatening to shatter the thing and kill her with its shards.

"Don't you hate how kids just love their parents and keep loving them, no matter what? Kids have no dignity that way, your parents fuck it all up and still you love them and love them, it's pitiful. Maybe there's nothing but happy little girl sunshine air inside your globe."

She tapped the beer can impatiently against the table. "Lay off my metaphor, ok?"

He reached again for her hand. She surrendered her arm limply. His skin was warm and dry and soft as a woman's.

When they arrived back at her apartment, Hillary's mother was in the bathroom. Half of the cheap food congealed around a wooden spoon in the pot.

The toilet flushed and her mother wandered out. "Who you got here?" she said, eyes wasted but voice steady.

"I'm on my way out," Alex said.

"No, sweetheart! Stay a while! It's so good for Hillary to have a friend, you know she just doesn't . . . what's that on your face?"

"It's an eyebrow ring, Mom," Hillary said.

Her mother's eyes drifted up and down Alex's body.

"Are you a boy?" she said. "Or a girl?" She gestured sloppily in Hillary's direction. "My daughter's a dyke, isn't that right, honey?" She looked around, swayed on her high heels. Sat down hard on the loveseat, spread her arms across the cushions. "It's okay to say 'dyke,' right?"

"Christ, Mom," Hillary said.

"What? Am I embarrassing you in front of your friend?" she said. "Am I making it all about *me*? Am I sucking up all the *air* in the *room*?"

Alex shrugged on his backpack, stuck out his hand in the direction of Hillary's mother. "Nice to meet you," he said.

Hillary's mother closed her eyes wearily, leaned her head back on the cushion. "Don't leave on my account. I'm about to pass out anyway. As Hillary will tell you." She exhaled heavily. "As Hillary tells everyone."

"I'm a boy," Alex said.

"I don't care what you are," Hillary told him.

Eyes closed, Hillary's mother snorted wetly. "Yes you do," she said.

"I don't!" Hillary said.

Alex wiped a sleeve on his face, smearing the sparkle makeup.

The infant next door started up its wailing. Alex reached for the doorknob, and Hillary's stomach lurched. The globe strained against its gaseous contents. Why must her mother always be in the room?

"Bye," Alex said, and was gone.

On Friday, Hillary took the CBS tour. The website promised a glimpse inside *The Price is Right* studio. Lurking at the edge of her gang of fifty tourists, Hillary's plan to peel off from the pack and slip inside Bob's Barker's dressing room seemed feasible enough, but the group turned out to be ringed on all sides by surly interns in ill-fitting suit jackets who yelled at her when she walked off the edge of the sidewalk, and again when she lingered at the ladies' room. They knew about people like her. They'd seen what Bob Barker's fans were capable of.

The following Monday, Hillary pulled a sage green T-shirt from her dresser. She ironed on the lettering herself, in her kitchen as her mother slept, using a kit she bought at a craft store. I LOVE BOB, it said. Elegant, she thought. Simple. She poured herself some of the vodka her mother brought home the night before. She drank it out of a paper cup, with ice and orange juice. It was early in the day, but so what. She lined the letters up straight and pressed down with patience, thinking dreamily about love and personal dignity and the ways in which they intersected and diverged.

She took a bus to the studio. This would be her new routine. She'd settle into a summer organized around standing in this line, going inside, trying to convince the same producers she was entertaining enough to Come on Down.

Los Angeles hummed. A woman in line behind her offered a chocolate donut, which tasted particularly good with the screwdrivers Hillary had brought in a plastic thermos she'd purchased that morning at Walgreen's for $5.89. The people around her were happy with anticipation. They were idiots, wearing shirts that erased their dignity, and she was one of them.

Around lunchtime she accepted another donut. Her thermos was empty. The sun caused a glare on the clean Los Angeles sidewalk as though in reflection off snow. Palm trees lining the street poked unnaturally up from the cement, their awful sharp leaves interrupting the sky.

"Honey?" The donut woman said. "You want to sit down?"

Hillary shook her head politely and then vomited the donuts and the vodka and orange juice, sullying the clean Los Angeles sidewalk and causing a flurry of caretaking activity by her fellow hopefuls. From inside the studio another grumpy intern emerged, and Hillary allowed herself to be led to a couch in the dim, cool office of an assistant producer. The intern placed a wastepaper basket on the floor next to her head and ordered her, without irony, to sleep it off.

She awoke to someone patting her forehead with damp paper towel.

"Atta girl," Bob Barker said. "Better? I was looking for Lorna but here you were."

He was as beautiful as she'd hoped. The familiarity of him, combined with the shock of his three-dimensional presence, hurt her eyes. "I'm sorry," she told him.

"Happens to the best of us." He was perched on the couch, next to her. His thigh was touching hers. His hand rested on the back of the sofa. Surely he didn't mean to make her feel this claustrophobic, but he seemed so huge. His body was a cage around her.

"Is this your office?"

"No," he chuckled. The same chuckle, the exact same little thing he did on television, the wry shake of the head. "Just hiding out."

"I don't drink, usually," she said.

"That much is clear." Again the chuckle. Sheets of Kleenex bloomed from his shirt collar. Up close, his skin wasn't as orange as she'd feared. Liver spots dotted the backs of his hands.

"I just wanted to see you, and I got drunk," Hillary said, stupidly. "I wanted to see you because I've been trying to see you and I've been watching you on TV."

"Easy," he told her. He took a sip from his coffee mug. His hand shook, just a little bit. Didn't he have somewhere else to be? The loose skin at his neck seemed to have been tucked into his collar.

With tremendous exertion Hillary sat upright. "I think you knew my mother," she said. "She won the Miss Orange County Pageant." Hillary burped, which helped her stomach a little. "In 1982. She says you're my father."

"Oh dear," he said.

"But then again, she's kind of a liar," Hillary said.

Hillary leaned over the pail, waiting to vomit again. As a little girl she'd spent nights waiting for her mother to come home from the bar. She'd hold all that shiny beauty queen hair out of the way as her mother leaned over the toilet. Hillary's own hair was now safe in a ponytail, neither shiny nor beautiful.

A person appeared in the doorway. "Mr. Barker," she said, in an exhale. "Bob."

He turned his head to the door, gazing mutely at the intruder.

"Two minutes," she told him.

"All righty," he said back. "Lorna," he explained to Hillary.

The woman didn't move from the doorway. She spoke into a walkie-talkie. "It's okay. I found him."

Bob Barker reached into his suit and pulled out a business card. "Call my manager," he said. "He handles these situations." Hillary brought the card to her nose. It smelled of cologne and cigarettes.

He snapped his fingers in recognition. "Joyce!" he said. "Was that her name?"

"Yes," Hillary said.

"Sweet girl. She walked my dogs."

"I knew it," Hillary said, deflated.

"I'm not the culprit, dear," Bob Barker said. "Got myself neutered in '79." He rose from the couch, and stood for a moment as if to find his balance. He crossed the room and opened a cabinet. "Here," he said, handing her a box wrapped in Christmas paper. "A parting gift."

Lorna stepped forward and took his elbow. "Sweetheart," he said to Lorna, in his rich television voice. "Call this young lady a cab, would you? Make sure she gets home."

"So long," Hillary said.

"Thanks for watching," he murmured.

When she reached the alley behind the studio, her legs still shaky, there was no cab. Lorna closed the stage door decisively behind her.

She waited. The alley was empty. Right now her mother would be back at the apartment, prone on the loveseat, legs dangling over the edge, wide awake. She'd be drinking, and worrying.

Hillary sweated, alone on the brilliant concrete. She found her phone at the bottom of her backpack and dialed. She removed the gift wrap from Bob's present.

"Hello?" Alex said. "Hillary? Is that you?"

"He gave me a board game!" she cried.

Behind her in the alley, a dumpster stood open. Its sugary acidic stench filled the Los Angeles afternoon. The sun burned on, baking her head. Inside her chest, the pottery globe shattered, piercing bone and muscle with its shrapnel and finally freeing her own sweet, childlike breath.

the steam room

helen was unhappily married to the mayor of their midsized American city. Sometimes she masturbated in the steam room of the downtown YMCA. A sign posted in the showers named the city statute under which those engaging in sexual behavior OF ANY KIND would be prosecuted. It admonished members to THINK! But yesterday afternoon, hidden in the semi-dark and wrapped in a hot fog, she called up the eyes of Johnny Depp, gazing into hers as his tongue traced perfect, slow circles around her clitoris.

The overhead light came on in a shocking flash of fluorescence. Two girls in City High School team swimsuits padded barefoot into the steam room and caught Helen deep in the throes of auto-arousal. Finding herself at the moment of orgasmic no return and unable to swallow her moan of release, she attempted to transform it into a protest, a shriek of warning:

what emerged was a yowl of ecstasy and mortification. *Don't,* she'd yelled throatily. *Don't come. In!*

The following morning as the political aftermath commenced, she was embarrassed more than anything else by the thought of herself slumped in the corner of the steam room: cellulite thighs, flabby midriff, sagging breasts. The newspaper referred to the girls—Jessica Nelson and Harper Lewis—as "the victims." But surely they were victimized more by the sight of her old-lady body than by what she'd been doing with her hand.

Jessica Nelson and Harper Lewis were after-school Bible Clubbers, vice-president and secretary, respectively, of the Youth Crew at First Christian Evangelical. Helen's daughter, Coral, went to school with them. Over a bowl of granola the next morning, Coral told Helen that despite their psychoChristian leanings, Jessica and Harper weren't exactly bitches. Helen let the profanity slide. A mother caught jilling off in public loses authority over such matters.

"Do I have to go to school today?" Coral asked.

"Yes," her father said.

"No," Helen said, simultaneously.

In the breakfast-nook sunlight, Coral's eyes were the color of their front lawn. She was a problematically beautiful child. Athletic, self-sustaining.

"Never mind," Coral said. "I have a math test."

She accepted a hug from her father. "Hang tough," Jerome told her, and kissed the top of her head.

Helen extended her hands to pull Coral into a hug, but her daughter shrugged on her backpack and walked a path around her, just out of arm's reach.

"Be brave," Helen said as the front door closed.

Jerome opened a jar peanut butter, put a spoonful in his mouth. "She's refusing to let it get to her."

"Put it on bread, for godsakes," Helen said. "Or a cracker." A month ago she told him she wanted a divorce. But he couldn't understand why she'd want to break up the family. He loved her, he said. But he was, after all, a politician, so she couldn't be sure how true that was. Regardless, divorce alienates churchgoers, and churchgoers constituted Jerome's loyal base. A population influx of newcomers from the liberal East Coast and the dismal performance of Jerome's party on the national scene meant his next campaign would need all hands on deck, including the city's popular first lady. For the sake of his career and for the advancement of their shared political agenda, Helen had decided, privately, to postpone leaving him until after the election.

Jerome pulled her into his chest. "It's all right," he told her. "We're managing the press. We've hired a hotdog public relations guy."

"This is how you spend my tax dollars?" His shirt muffled her. The smell of peanut butter was nauseating. "Never mind. I'm sorry," Helen told him.

He pulled away from her. "As you've mentioned."

"But you don't believe it."

He licked his spoon again. "Believe what?"

Helen shook her head and turned to face the sink. She twisted the faucet and watched the water land hard against the breakfast dishes.

"The campaign starts in January," he said.

"I know exactly when the campaign starts." She'd been through enough of them by now to know the routine. Gathering signatures, canvassing neighborhoods in the sweltering heat, making sandwiches for volunteers, shopping for dresses to attend more banquet dinners. Showing up, because Jerome's poll numbers rose when she did. Not that her values or even her personality were responsible for her popularity numbers, which were higher even than his. It was all in the hair and the wardrobe. And in the fund-raising, the fund-raising.

Television reporters were camped on the street in front of her house and a police cruiser was parked in her driveway. Helen moved the curtain aside with her finger. One of the photographers jumped from his lawn chair and pointed his lens at the house.

At lunchtime, Lynne, the CEO of Girls' House, showed up at Helen's back door, carrying Chinese takeout. Helen was one of Lynne's board members. Over the past decade she'd raised hundreds of thousands of dollars to keep homeless girls off the streets, out of the strip clubs, safe from sexually abusive fathers and cousins and teachers. "Your neighbor let me climb over her wall," Lynne said. "I wasn't about to run that gauntlet in your front yard."

Behind her, neighbor Diane waved. "Lousy rotten deal, Helen!" she yelled from her side of the wall. "I have a lasagna in the oven for you!"

Over lunch, Helen told Lynne she'd be resigning from the board. "You'll come back after a while," Lynne said. Helen gave them both a break and didn't say what each of them knew; that over the course of the coming year they could count on a percentage of Helen's donors politely declining to renew their gifts. It meant something for Lynne to have come, sneaking in the back door notwithstanding. In doing so she risked certain accusations. Sympathizing with a predator, for example.

A predator! Those girls had walked in on *her*.

They ate their Chinese and talked for a while, about moral hypocrisies and false standards of decency and what girls are taught to believe. All those strategy meetings and donor lunches they'd been through together, yet Helen had never suspected Lynne's opinions were so much in synch with her own. Helen was both comforted and mildly surprised when Lynne admitted she was not, strictly speaking, quite as *heterosexual* as she'd led people to believe.

"Do you have a girlfriend?" Helen asked.

"I'm so closeted I've got dust bunnies in my hair." She poked fiercely at her lo mein with a chopstick. "Yeah, no girlfriend. Any woman who could abide all this lying would be too fucked up even for me."

Helen's son, Chax, called. "Don't make me talk to you about this," Helen said. Chax was in his freshman year at an enormous state university one hundred miles away. He lived in a grungy fraternity house.

"The AP picked it up," he said. "It's on the CNN website. You're human interest, congratulations."

"I'm sorry, honey," Helen said. She was catching up on laundry. Folding underwear, matching socks. Coral's brassieres were becoming harder to distinguish from Helen's own.

"Next it'll be Letterman." Chax was a political science major. A while ago he admitted to her he'd rather be studying English literature. He hadn't yet figured out a way to tell his father.

"He creeps me out," Helen said. "Can't I have Leno?"

"This isn't really that funny, Mom."

"And if it were someone else's mother?" She folded one of Jerome's undershirts. Even in the thick of public humiliation, one could rely on certain household constants. She wanted badly to tell Chax she was planning to divorce his father. She needed an ally. If this made her a rotten mother, then so be it. Coral would take Jerome's side, no question. She'd know in an instant that Helen was the instigator.

"Should I come home?" Chax said.

Helen recalled the pile of dirty laundry he'd brought with him last time. "And do what? Have a nice family talk about masturbation?"

"Was that you trying to shock me?"

"I can't get my mother out of my mind," she told him. "I've been thinking about her all day, your grandma, about what it meant to be raised in the orphanage, by the nuns. Do you know last lucid thing she said to me, just before the dementia completely took over? She said, 'just make sure they keep my pootie clean.'"

"Remember that summer we went to the lake?" Chax said. "With the Clynes and the Baxters?"

Helen remained silent. Here it came: another revelation about the ways in which she'd failed him as a mother. College brought out the worst in one's kids.

"Remember Amy Baxter?" Chax said. "She was seventeen?"

Helen made a sound. "Self-absorbed?" she said. "High on pot most of the time?"

He sighed, that exasperated noise he'd been making at her since he was little. "All right," she said. "What about her? What about Amy Baxter?" The folding was done. She was ready to hang up.

"She used to do it in her bedroom with the curtain open," Chax said.

"Masturbate?" Helen slid down to the floor, her back against the wall. "You were how old? Twelve?"

"It doesn't really matter."

"Did she know you were watching?" Helen said.

"Christ," he mumbled. "That hadn't occurred to me."

"Why are you telling me this, Chax? Now?"

"Huh," he said. "Good question."

On her way back to the kitchen from distributing her family's clothing in dressers and closets, Helen glanced out the back window and spotted her neighbor, Diane, sitting atop the back wall, her legs dangling over to Helen's side. She was holding a casserole dish in her lap and examining her fingernails.

"Save me!" she said, when Helen came outside. "I'm in limbo!"

Helen fetched a stepstool from the utility shed. "My legs are so short!" Diane said. She handed the lasagna down to Helen.

"Wow," Helen said. "Dinner. And not even a death in the family."

"What else am I going to do?" Diane said. She climbed down. "Food, support, whatever." She looked around. "Nice garden."

"You want some coffee?" Helen said, resigned. Diane would not be denied the chance to venture into the mayor's house.

In the kitchen she peeked through the mini-blinds to Helen's front yard. "Good Lord," Diane said.

"Slow news day," Helen said.

"I put sausage in the lasagna. I hope you aren't a vegetarian!"

Helen really didn't like people all that much. They required such effort. Diane pulled at her ear, rubbed her knee. She looked at Helen expectantly.

"How are your boys?" Helen said. She couldn't remember their names. The older one had been riding the school bus with Coral for a dozen years.

"The same!" Diane said. "Obnoxious, you know. Boys. Sex! My god, the things you need to tell them. Frankie, who's turning seven? We try to educate him. We give him books—"

"Books?" Helen said. When Coral and Chax were kids, she'd just sat them down, tried not to grimace too much, and talked at them until no one could stand it anymore. "Who gives him the books, you or your husband?"

Diane blew on her coffee, tongued it tentatively. "Santa."

"So how is your husband?" Helen said. "Tony, right?" Diane's tics were making Helen jittery.

"Good, good. Fine. Working too much. Horrible, actually. I never see him. I'm not exactly an exciting draw anymore, to tell you the truth. To get him home."

Helen looked at the clock. Coral would be home from school in about ten minutes. "Sounds hard," she said.

"You have no idea!" Diane said. "We haven't had sex in," she held up her hands. "Five days. At least."

Lately, Helen and Jerome were as chaste as siblings. Except that he still got undressed in front of her. Hoping, she supposed, that she'd notice the effects of his new exercise regimen. Such a shame, she thought. He started to look good the moment she could no longer stand the thought of fucking him.

"I suppose I could spice it up," Diane said. "What do you know about sex toys?"

"Not a thing."

"Because there's this vibrating rabbit thing, or bunny I guess you'd call it—" The phone rang. Helen jumped to answer it.

"I like to watch," said a voice.

The skin covering her old-lady body prickled. How surprising that it could still produce the electricity necessary for gooseflesh.

"Was your day a living hell, honey?" Helen asked Coral when she arrived home.

"Yes, Helen, it pretty much was," Coral replied. Out of her backpack she pulled a page from a magazine, folded into a tiny square. "Found this in my locker," she said, and unfolded a centerfold photo. A dark-haired woman was spread-eagled on a bale of hay, her head thrown back, tongue on her upper teeth, gazing into the camera. Touching herself, naturally. How itchy that hay must be against her skin, thought Helen.

"Oh God, sweetheart," Helen said. There were times she felt the impulse to stop whatever she was doing and change the world, immediately. Most often this feeling occurred when she was ovulating. It had been a long while, though, since that need had come over her. Perhaps this was a clue that menopause lurked just around the bend.

"I'm supposed to be really angry at you, right?" Coral said. "I'm supposed to make you feel like shit?" She dropped her backpack on the kitchen floor and opened the refrigerator. "Or I'm supposed to go bad, like take Ecstasy and smoke pot and start having sex with girls."

Helen inhaled. "How about I just buy you a car and we'll call it even?"

"Go ahead, make fun," Coral said.

"I'm sorry, honey," Helen told her.

"I'm going to my room to smoke cigarettes," Coral said.

"I remember high school," Helen said desperately. "I remember how people were!" Last semester, the school's swim coach came on to Coral. He'd been allowed to leave his job quietly, his credentials permanently revoked, in an agreement devised to protect Coral from the intensity of a local news media hungry for scandal involving the city's elite. If it weren't for Coral's feelings, Helen would have backed a public lynching. The creep had so deftly slithered his way into poor Coral's head—he'd had her believing he was in love with her, of all ridiculous things—that she'd begged them not to embarrass him, to let the whole thing go. So they did.

And now, six months later, the poor kid was burdened by this sin of her mother's. Were it not for Jerome's job, nobody would have cared what Helen did in the steam room, or that yet another swim coach turned out to be a sick predatory asshole. Thanks to Jerome's narcissistic career choice, her sweet child was enduring high school with sexual scandals bobbing over her head like Pooh's raincloud. But adoring her father as she did, Coral would keep her misery to herself. Not so Helen: she'd made it shriekingly clear to Jerome that she was sick to death of being held accountable to backroom powermongers, corporate newspaper hawkers, and throngs of adoring, wild-eyed, political junkies.

"Right, right." Coral mimicked a blabbing mouth with her hand. "High school sucks. And when I run into Jessica and Harper at our ten-year reunion they'll be fat, with a hundred kids and jobs at Walmart." She turned away and clumped up the steps in her heavy shoes.

Helen knew better than to go after her, to impose a conversation. When Coral was little she'd been a snuggler, crawling into Helen's lap, climbing into bed, resting her little head in the hollow of Helen's shoulder. When had she stopped doing that? When was the last time she had cuddled this child? She resisted the urge to chase Coral upstairs, hug her hard. At some point, a mother's blundering love turns a child into an adversary.

Jerome was advised by the city's public relations consultant not to appear on camera with Helen. "I'll be right here," he said, standing at the fireplace. Their living room was full of people: Jerome's aides, the PR guy, the news cameraman, a reporter from Channel 9, and Helen's hairdresser, who'd cancelled his afternoon appointments and shown up at her house with a bottle of white wine, his makeup kit, and a story about his first sexual encounter, at age thirteen, with his best friend Bobby. He and Bobby had engaged in clumsy, embarrassing, and unsafe sex in their junior high school band practice room while the rest of the student body watched Bobby's twin brother win the regional spelling bee championship.

Helen gripped a blue index card that Jerome had brought home from the office. *My actions were inappropriate,* it said. *I did not intend to cause anyone pain or discomfort. I extend my deepest apologies to the two young women and their parents.* Trying to be funny, Jerome told her these three sentences cost the city $250 a word in consulting fees.

The PR guy spent ninety minutes, before the reporter arrived, coaching Helen and repeating that she was going to do great. Nothing in his demeanor or tone suggested he believed this. Time was spent arranging Helen on the couch. The PR guy placed a family photo on the end table at her elbow. He coaxed their elderly cocker spaniel onto Helen's lap. Her hairdresser poked at the top of her head.

"Hang on," the reporter said. "Mrs. uh, Mayor?" she pointed a manicured hand toward the staircase. "May I . . . ? Your bathroom?"

Jerome sighed. The PR guy cleared his throat, tugged at his tie. Helen led the reporter upstairs to her master bathroom. She sat on the edge of her bed to wait. Inside, the faucet opened and water ran uninterrupted, a flow of white noise, a cover for something else. Helen listened for a while, then knocked.

"Hello?" she said. She couldn't remember the woman's name. "Everything okay?"

"Oh, God," the reporter said. Her voice was close; she must have been sitting with her back to the door. "I just needed to take a minute."

The water ran on. Helen had installed the low-flow attachment herself last year. It made a column of water and tiny air bubbles that resulted in a controlled unnatural exhale, a sanitized splash against the porcelain.

"How old are you, anyway?" Helen said to the door.

She heard the reporter take a long, deep breath. "I slept with my boss," she said. "About an hour ago." There was no hint of tears in her voice. Helen heard the thud of the reporter's head as she rested it against the hollow door. "I was at the top of my class at Cornell," the reporter said. "Now all I really want is a shower."

"Go ahead, then," Helen said. "Let them wait."

"I'll just wash up." She grunted, presumably to her feet.

"Hang on," Helen said. "Let me get you a washcloth."

When the reporter cracked open the door, Helen averted her eyes and slipped the cloth inside. She felt a firm, sisterly squeeze of appreciation on her fingers.

Neighbor Diane's lasagna was dry, and made with sauce from a jar. Jerome ate two portions. Coral rose from the table and peeked through the blinds. "The yard is still full of loonies," she said.

They stood on their front porch, the three of them. A handful of people in lawn chairs held candles and stared back. Two of the women grasped a banner. Quilted in scrap fabric appeared the message THE WAGES OF SIN ARE DEATH. "Got to hand it to them." Jerome said. "Those ladies are quick with the sewing machine."

"Look, it's Jessica and Harper's parents," Coral said. Helen examined their plain, lined foreheads, soft double chins, crow's feet. These were honest faces, fearful and resolute.

On both sides, their neighbors also stood on porches. The kids across the street sat cross-legged on the lawn, staring. Everyone here owned a beautiful house. Helen looked around at them, the people to whom she'd loaned pairs of eggs and cups of milk, for whom she'd baked casseroles, with whom she'd painted fences, weeded communal plots, argued over covenants and restrictions. They too were decent people. In the pink evening light they were attractive and healthy-looking. They met her gaze; offered bewildered waves, rueful grins. One by one they turned away and went inside their homes.

On the ten o'clock news, Helen came off chastened but calm. She smiled with sufficient humility. The district attorney was interviewed. It was too early, he said, to decide whether to prosecute.

The PR guy was still there. He removed his sweat-stained suit jacket and accepted a tumbler of bourbon from Jerome. "Right after my divorce," he said, "I got busted screwing my new girlfriend on the Sheep's Meadow in Central Park. It was three a.m. The cop was on horseback, snuck right up on us. Scared the shit out of me." He grinned at them. By next week, this guy would be entertaining his hipster friends with the story of a political wife's misfortune and the mastery with which he spun it away.

By eleven o'clock, the candlelight vigilantes were packing up their lawn chairs. Helen watched them from the bedroom upstairs, the light extinguished. Jerome lay on the bedspread in the dark. Helen knew these people, most of them. Two years ago she had attended a PTA potluck at the Nelsons'. Crosses were hung on every wall, but the family didn't come off as zealots.

The last minivan pulled away and the street quieted. All Helen had left to look at was her own weak reflection in the glass. She left the window and lay down on the bedspread next to her husband.

"They're just trying to raise their kids, you know?" she said.

"I should have been there with you on the couch," he said. "You shouldn't have had to do that interview alone." He reached for her hand.

She got up from the bed. "It wasn't your most courageous hour."

"Do you have any idea of the damage you've done?" In the dim light his profile raised up, elbows on the mattress. "Helen? Do you? If I lose the election, the downtown stadium project goes down the tubes. Not to mention the light rail proposal. That's thirty million dollars in private development right there."

"In other words, I had an expensive orgasm."

"You fucked up, Helen."

"I was unlucky," she said.

"You were reckless."

"Fine. So I fucked up. I'm sorry. I fucked up. Looks like you've lost your star fundraiser."

"Don't assume the DA won't come after you," Jerome said. "He's up for reelection too, you know. And forgive me if this feels a little bit like sabotage."

"This again," Helen said.

"You signed up for it." He stood from the bed and pulled aside the curtain. The outside air felt clammy against her skin. Finally the street was quiet. "This is public life. This is how it works."

Twelve years ago, a clutch of party elders, including their congressman, came to the house. She made them coffee. Somebody brought a lemon pound cake baked by his wife. They told Jerome that this town needed a mayor with some common sense and a good public face. The congressman brightly reminded Helen of the perks: her public duties would land her a closetful of new dresses.

Helen rooted through the papery detritus accumulating on their dresser. "Where the hell are my driving glasses?"

Jerome rubbed his hands over his face, a condescending gesture. "The YMCA, Helen? For Christ's sake! All those kids running around? All those old people?"

"Don't forget the cripples," she said.

"Irresponsibility—"

"Wait! I get it. I have orgasms without you!" She clapped her hand to her chest. "That's it, isn't it? I got myself off. Nobody respects a candidate whose wife—"

"Has a criminal record?"

She found her glasses and put them on. The streetlight outside the window shone behind him, the backlight erasing his features. "Don't think it's not a sickening feeling," she confessed. "I'm sickened."

As Helen backed the car out of the garage, Coral appeared in the driveway. She was in her bathrobe, barefoot. Her eyes were swollen. "Sweetie," Helen said. "What is it?"

"Where are you going?"

"For a drive." The garage door was open, the light blaring into the neighborhood.

"Can I come?"

"I was thinking of going to see the girls' parents," Helen said.

"Right now?" Coral said. The clock on the wall of the garage read five minutes to midnight.

"Well," Helen said.

"What will you say to them?"

"I don't know, love," Helen told her.

"Can't we just get some ice cream?"

They took their cones to the municipal golf course. Coral showed her a hole in the chain link. "Kids from school come here," she said. "But you've got to do it barefoot."

She tucked her sandals neatly against the fence. "I did this when I was your age."

They sat in the sand trap near the sixteenth green. In the hollows of the course, a soft, warm mist was gathering. Tiny bird tracks ran through the cool sand.

"I'm divorcing your father," Helen said.

Coral stood, and ran from the sand trap. She hurled her ice cream cone into the dark. Helen groaned to her feet and followed her daughter, jogging down the dewy sloping green hill to the southern end of the course, toward the eucalyptus trees. When Helen caught up, Coral was sitting in the tall grass, her hands over her eyes, weeping.

"How stupid can you be?" Coral said.

"I made a mistake. I was angry at your dad. Maybe—"

"That's not what I mean!" Coral cried.

"Oh my God," Helen said, searching her child's eyes. "The swim coach?"

Helen knew it, maybe she'd known it all along. His lies about love would have gotten Coral to take off her Speedo. Helen clutched at her daughter, pulled her into an embrace. In the distance a police siren wailed. Here was her child, her second-born, her tough little girl.

They sank to the ground, into the brush bordering the fairway, and lay entwined for a while under the municipal sky. The tall grass bent and swayed at the edge of the bed they'd pressed into the rough. Coral nestled her head into the hollow of Helen's shoulder as the light fog rolled over them like steam, obscuring the stars.

juniper beach

harlie works as an auto travel counselor in the Cranston, Rhode Island, branch office of the American Automobile Association. Mostly her job involves the assembly of Trip-Tiks. Charlie's parents are newly dead, their car having run off the road three weeks ago outside of Tucson, Arizona. Upon her return to work after their funeral, she began creating TripTiks that send Triple-A members to destinations different than those they requested.

There have been complaints. But this week Charlie rescued a pair of newlyweds from a vulgar Niagara Falls weekend, sending them instead on an off-season bargain honeymoon in the turret of a renovated French Canadian chateau overlooking Lake Ontario. Yesterday a father showed up at her counter hoping a White Mountains fishing trip would separate his teenage sons from their Xboxes; Charlie saved him from KOA campground monotony and sent him and the boys to a grouping of national forest log cabins on the Tioga River.

The TripTik request form now at the top of Charlie's inbox has been completed by Ruth and Geoffrey Leaf, who report that they would like to travel to Orlando. They have reserved a premium campsite at the Disney Fort Wilderness Resort. The brochure Mrs. Leaf attached to the Request Form, presumably as a caution against Charlie being unable to find Disney World on a map, described the campground's recent improvements, including "enlarged paving in many sites." Charlie tosses the brochure into her wastebasket. If Ruth and Geoffrey Leaf carry out their plans, the Leaf children will not, during this vacation, run squealing into the waves of the great and friendly Atlantic. They will not bite into tuna sandwiches gritty with sand. They will not squint into the clear sky and engage in thrilling speculation about Gulf Coast hurricanes.

A TripTik consists of a series of map strips on narrow slips of paper. If you clipped a particular section of American interstate—fifty miles, say—out of a typical road map and enlarged it tenfold, you'd have a Trip-Tik strip. Each strip opens like a pamphlet and has a map detail inside, showing popular landscape features, human-made monuments, secondary roads.

Charlie pulls strips of map from their cubbyholes, creating a little pile, and sits down at her desk. She runs her orange highlighter over the interstate. At the end of each strip she draws an arrowhead to redundantly indicate that it's time to turn the page. Charlie's mother used to say that one mustn't take a paycheck for granted. Charlie twirls the rubber stamp carousel on her desk, plucks off the stamp that says Speed Limit Rigidly Enforced and thumps it onto strip C-122, between exits fourteen and seven in southern Georgia, where the interstate crosses Rose Creek Swamp. In fifty-one years, Charlie's mother never earned a dollar she could call her own. She died when Charlie's father, traveling drunk at top speed on a perfectly straight road in the shadow of a place called Tumamoc Hill, ended their vacation by driving their tinny rented Ford Fiesta into a two-hundred-year-old giant saguaro cactus, top-heavy with six tons of monsoon-season moisture. It collapsed onto the car, crushing it. It would be nice if the circumstances of her parents' death did not remind her of a scene from a Wile E. Coyote cartoon, but she keeps imagining the Road Runner, wicked witness to all manner of coyote injury, speeding from the scene.

The Leaf family will take Interstate 95, straight south. At least for a while, 95 is the New Jersey Turnpike, but there's a tricky exit where it intersects with 287: Mr. Leaf will need to make a quick left-lane merge, otherwise he'll end up on Route 440 to Perth Amboy and into a nightmare of auxiliary roads. Charlie turns to the map detail on the inside of the strip and draws a loop to demonstrate how to navigate this cloverleaf. After this point, it's smooth sailing, as long as Mr. Leaf watches the signs. Nobody really needs a TripTik to get to Disney World. But to know your route is a comfort, a pleasure, a bit of security. Charlie finds nothing wrong with her desire to minister to those with an impaired sense of direction. A good map tells you where you are, where you're going, and where you've been.

Via highlighter, she diverts the Leaf family to Juniper Beach. At Juniper Beach, oceanside cottages painted in pastel overlook the sea. They are equipped with Formica dinette sets and 1950s iceboxes, only slightly rusted around the edges, and Adirondack chairs on the porch meant for sipping rum mojitos in the slanted evening light while chicken with jerk sauce roasts on the grill and pink-skinned kids wreak mischief with water balloons. At Juniper Beach there are no super-smooth roller coasters or six-dollar hot dogs.

Although rolling in money—the degree to which Charlie learned only after their deaths—her parents believed in accomplishing family road trips via the cheap, old-fashioned purity of the American station wagon;

the state park campground; the family-owned roadside diner. Her father took back roads when he could and interstates only at night: darkened two-lane highways were overrun with Indians and drunken rednecks, especially west of the Mississippi. "During the day those types stay in bed with their hangovers," he said.

Before she turned to guerrilla travel planning, Charlie spent six years politely suggesting stimulating vacation alternatives to Triple-A customers. She pointed out secondary highways to nature preserves, trails through state parks, roadside curiosities. She shared scenery, historical interest, local quirks she remembered from a childhood strung together by road trips. Members would lean on the counter as she talked. They would touch the map with their fingertips. "But if you could get us straight to Miami Beach . . . ?" they'd say. They'd open a Tour Book, search for a Holiday Inn. Most often they were focused on the availability of high-speed internet access and of discount coupons to Sea World.

When Charlie is done marking the strips for the Leaf family, she takes the pile to the back of the room and places them between glossy cardstock covers bearing the Triple-A logo. Recently the Triple-A research and development department launched web-based software that allows members to make their own TripTiks online. Charlie slips a plastic spine onto the binder machine and pulls the lever to open the comb. She works the die cuts at the top of each strip onto the row of curved plastic prongs. You can't create a book on your personal computer. You can't access professional expertise. An internet TripTik is nothing more than a sheaf of office paper cluttering up your car. It doesn't even fit in the glove box.

Charlie and her girlfriend Heather have been together for six years. They are headed for dissolution, a fact Heather seems unable to face.

"You're in shock," Heather says. "Don't make any big decisions right now." She pushes Charlie's bangs off her forehead. Which is an annoyance, given that her forehead is the area over which Charlie wants her bangs to fall.

"Small decisions aren't doing the job," Charlie says. She removes herself from the couch, from Heather's proximity. Charlie is feeling emotionally ungenerous. Heather discovered this phrase in a book entitled *Making Same-Sex Relationships Work*. But ever since a cactus crushed Charlie's parents, the term has disappeared from Heather's vocabulary, along with negative sentiments generally. Whatever interesting edginess that existed in Heather's personality has disappeared. She has become a gusher of positivism, upbeat affirmations, gentle and kind and philosophical. She offers resources.

"There's humor in it, you realize," Charlie says. "Honestly, a saguaro? It's slapstick."

"It's okay," Heather says. "You should laugh if it would help."

"Haven't you always wondered about the children of people who died doing something stupid?" Charlie says. "Can you imagine? Going back to sixth grade and sitting there in math class, everyone knowing your father broke his neck diving into shallow water?"

"Nobody was doing anything stupid," Heather says. She strokes anxious finger furrows into the pelt of their German shepherd, Ralph. "Except driving drunk, I guess."

At the funeral, Charlie's brother had downed a six-pack in their parents' kitchen and informed her that the old man had become pretty much a full-time drunk starting the Easter Sunday when *standing on this very linoleum* she announced she was in love with a woman.

"Quit being an asshole," Charlie said. They both knew that their parents had turned out to be crazy about Heather. They saw her as a positive influence on their gloomy kid.

He stared into his bottle for a minute, crying some more. "I'll quit being an asshole when you quit being a queer."

"I guess that makes you pretty much a permanent asshole," she told him.

When Charlie gets back to her desk from her lunch break, she unwraps a new Triple-A members-only free-gift tote bag from its plastic. Inside she places her lunchbox, her spare shoes and toothbrush, and the personal effects on her desk, detritus of summers past: a framed photo of herself at the rim of the Grand Canyon, taken when she was four; a petrified rock paperweight from Utah; a tiny but authentic Hopi Indian basket in which she keeps change for the soda machine; a carved wooden mermaid purchased at an artists' cooperative on a rainy day in Asheville, North Carolina.

She packages the TripTik for Ruth and Geoffrey Leaf together with large regional foldout maps of the northeastern and southeastern United States, upon which she's convincingly marked the route they requested, the route to Disney nirvana. This, Charlie hopes, together with their trust in Triple-A, will ease them into the complacency required to accept that she, their auto travel counselor, possesses certain pieces of knowledge; to accept with only the briefest moment of confusion (perhaps even shrugging in a way not unlike lemmings might, if lemmings had shoulders) that the best access to Orlando comes by way of Juniper Beach.

Because members always flip to the back of their TripTik to check the destination—who can resist a destination?—Charlie has finished the Leafs' booklet with the strip of map that contains Disney World. She has omitted, however, the piece that would get them there from Juniper Beach. For good measure—and in defiance of Triple-A policy—she has written a cheerful *Have a Great Vacation!* in heavy black marker over a critical section of the southeastern U.S. regional map, obscuring the route away from Juniper Beach. She places the Leaf family vacation plans in the Completeds drawer. Ruth Leaf will arrive tomorrow to pick it up.

With the Leafs' TripTik finished and her boss in the parking lot with his afternoon beers, Charlie begins a scrapbook containing automobile fatalities. She clips articles from the newspaper or prints them from the internet. On a slick curve in remote Highway 2, fifty miles southeast of Billings, Montana, a pair of teenagers, twin sons of a single mother who raised them on her salary as a rural paramedic, rolled their Toyota pickup. The twin in the passenger seat was thrown through the windshield. It took the ambulance thirty-five minutes to arrive, and when it did, the mother performed CPR on her dead son for another forty. The other twin, the driver, survived unhurt.

A retired couple on vacation near Puerto Peñasco, Mexico, hit a truck carrying firewood head-on at sixty miles per hour on a dark stretch of MR 8, twenty minutes south of the border. The husband had attempted to pass a Volkswagen bus on an uphill curve. The kind local woman driving the VW, knowing the *federales* routinely imprison *turistas* who cause accidents until insurance paperwork is filed and authenticated, put the stunned and bleeding *Americana* into her car and drove her away, leaving the husband's body on the side of the road.

Charlie glues the articles onto pages and snaps them into a three-ring binder that she's gutted of the Triple-A employee handbook. She finds the spot on a TripTik strip where each accident happened and she marks a cross in pink highlighter. She pastes these strips next to the articles.

That night, she takes Ralph to a new car dealership. It is midnight. She parks her fifteen-year-old Hyundai on a side street and steps over a knee-high gate. She's come in the dead of night to avoid the car salesmen. Ralph sniffs the curb at the edge of the lot. Charlie and her brother each received $72,000 in life insurance money from their parents. More will arrive when the estate settles. She and the dog stroll up and down the aisles. Under the neon floodlights, the cars sparkle. Broken glass, or mica, something shiny, has been mixed into the asphalt. Ralph's aluminum tags clink together cheerfully, although the air is clammy with moisture and gnats.

Someone is employed here whose job description is to wash and shine all these vehicles. Whoever it is takes pride in his work. Still, the cars fail to dazzle her. They hulk malevolently in their spaces, a grid of death machines.

On the way home, she spots a miniature RV parked under a yellow streetlamp in a vacant lot. A banner made from a bedsheet says FOR SALE. It is now one o'clock in the morning. She circles the RV, finds herself actually kicking the tires. She climbs the front bumper and peers inside: compact, economical. Blue plush. The front seat is like a recliner. She calls the number on the banner. When she mentions she can pay cash, the owner stops squawking over having been awakened.

"Are you breaking up with me?" Heather asks when Charlie climbs down.

"Not really," Charlie tells her.

"Just because you're experiencing a loss doesn't mean you get to treat me badly," Heather says.

"For once I wish you would just be clear. Don't you mean I can't be a bitch simply because my parents are dead?"

"Sweetie," Heather replies. "Isn't that what I just said?"

A family of three, driving through Yellowstone National Park, pulled over to watch a brown bear and her cubs. The mother bear approached their car, reared up on her hind legs, and sniffed at the groceries inside the car-top carrier. Excited, the parents unbuckled their seat belts for a better view. A tourist bus with a distracted driver sideswiped the car, plunging them into a ravine. The infant daughter, still strapped into a rear-facing child safety seat installed by trained firemen, was the only survivor.

From Cranston, Rhode Island, one's interstate options are limited to north or south. After you've gone south for a while, your choices expand significantly. Charlie takes I-95 through New London, switches to 287 in Westchester and heads over the Tappan Zee Bridge, turning south toward New Jersey. Just north of Parsippany she changes to I-80 and settles in for the straight, unchallenging haul lengthwise across Pennsylvania. The seat in her RV cradles her so comfortably it's a hazard: a person could fall asleep.

Charlie is halfway surprised to find actual scenery outside her enormous windshield: purple mountains, fruited plains, et cetera. The TripTik would have you believe these sixty miles contain only an expanse of flat, white nothing. TripTik page R-33, which covers this stretch of highway, was a filler strip, a connector through which her highlighter used to race, uninterrupted, to the next turnoff.

She passes exits for state parks: Ricketts Glen, Little Pine, Cook Forest, Oil Creek. She crosses the Susquehanna, the Allegheny. She planned to stop for the night at Shenango River Lake, six miles off the interstate, which according to her Tour Book features a number of campsites overlooking the water. Nearby is an 1854 Greek Revival mansion, renovated to mimic Tara in *Gone with the Wind*. Tour guides wear Civil War–era costumes. Charlie is tired, though, too tired to drive on.

Summer 1996, central New Hampshire: in a rare moment of sibling unity, Charlie and her brother conspired to wheedle their parents into a KOA campground for the night. "They've got pinball machines," her brother said. "And a lounge with a TV."

"*Friends* is on tonight," Charlie said.

"No dice," their father said. They ended up gazing, heavy-lidded, at the stars through an open skylight in the vaulted ceiling of a Forest Service knotty pine cabin, exhausted from an evening of chasing crickets, tossing pinecones into a blazing campfire, and skipping flat rocks into the water as a full orange moon rose over the Tioga.

Charlie sleeps in the parking lot of a Burger King at exit 4A in West

Middlesex, at the intersection of State Route 60. In the morning she sits at the RV's fold-down table and watches the sun rise over a strip mall. She expected to feel different. She expected to know more about where she is going. She consumes a paper cup of coffee; a sausage, egg, and cheese Croissan'wich; and French Toast sticks, which she dips one by one into a tiny plastic tub of delicious imitation maple syrup.

On a breathtaking stretch of the Alaska Highway, thirty-four miles southeast of Tok, three brothers on a summer road trip from Portland discovered the beer in their cooler was growing warm. They encountered a glacier they judged to be within climbing distance. On his way back to their Jeep, a four-pound chunk of prehistoric ice in his backpack, one of the brothers slid down the rocky hill and broke his ankle. As the others were carrying him across the road, a logging truck emerged around the bend. To avoid hitting the men, the driver plunged his truck over the cliff and was killed on impact.

Charlie keeps to the interstate. She stops at outlet malls, strip malls, shopping malls, multiplexes, big box superstores, franchise restaurants. She is in America: it is the same everywhere. Before the trip she hadn't appreciated the beauty of this monoculture. Like her father, she was disdainful, judgmental. But here in this America, everything is clean. Neon signs are never missing their letters. Toilets flush. Restrooms sport maintenance charts encased in plastic, employee initials indicating the frequency with which traces of human biology have been wiped away. Food arrives quickly and is hot or crispy, soft or cold, as appropriate, packaged in paper, delivered on clean plates by servers in the same uniform as the place eighty miles ago. At cinema multiplexes adjoining five-lane highways, she watches movies of minimal artistic merit. She saves the popcorn bag in Akron and smuggles it in for a free refill in Cleveland. She is at home in

America, rootless yet ensconced, held in place by her movement across strips of landscape.

Charlie affixes a map of the contiguous United States to the wall above her bed in the RV. She records her progress each day with a blue highlighter. Behind the wheel, she ponders the notions of equal opportunity and freedom of mobility and such American proverbs as *Home is where the heart is* and *Everything happens for a reason.*

The sun sets over Oklahoma wheat fields. Her windshield is bug-splattered. Ahead, she spots a Denny's sign rising fifty feet into the pink prairie sky. Some camping mornings, when they were up with the sun and her mother said she couldn't stand to cook one more meal at another dirt campsite, they'd leave their tent pitched, their equipment at the site, and drive to town for a greasy spoon breakfast. Their father would order tomato juice and ask the waitress for Worcestershire and mustard and a lemon wedge and a stalk of celery. Other diners would look sideways at him, grin when the vodka appeared from his coat pocket. In a shmoozing voice that would mortify Charlie, he'd offer to mix up a few for the people in the next booth.

The detail inside the TripTik strip for the hundred-mile stretch of southwest Montana is clear and accurate, in keeping with Triple-A standards. Charlie locates the stretch of road where the twins died. She'd have preferred to be there at night, to drive the S-curve in the dark like the boys did. She parks at the opening of a long dirt road, the RV straddling a cattle guard. She's purchased a Polaroid at a Target somewhere. The sky is cloudless; asphalt snakes away into mountain foothills. The twins must have ridden this curve a thousand times in the back seat of their mother's car. She would have warned them, when they got their learners' permits, to exercise caution here. She might have instructed them about the moment at which a good driver accelerates through a turn. She might have railed against the landowners who refused to grant right-of-way to the state, requiring road builders to construct a nonsensical corner on an otherwise straight prairie road. She might have told them stories about her own high school friends crashing their cars here. The boys would have rolled their eyes.

Charlie walks the road. The accident occurred eight months ago. The weeds have regrown, skid marks have worn away, bloodstains long gone or scrubbed off the pavement by some rancher's wife. The paint on the wooden memorial marker has begun to flake. Water has seeped between the plastic laminate protecting the boys' photo. Charlie takes a picture and stands at the side of the road, waiting for it to develop. She is eighty-six miles from the nearest interstate.

Near Boise she stops at a Kinko's. Three hundred emails fill the screen, mostly junk. Eight are from Heather; one for each day Charlie's been gone. She prints them and pays the cashier fifty cents per page.

There are miles and miles of road; thousands, potentially millions. There is friendliness on the highway; reliability. Weeks can be lost in the hum of tires, in the movement of the sun across the sky. In the traffic, the vacationers, the eighteen-wheelers, the traveling salesmen. Roadside, wildflowers blur into brushstrokes of yellow on the prairie, blue in the mountains, white everywhere. The RV runs; it drinks its gasoline, its wiper fluid, its oil; excretes its exhaust, its gray water, its sewage. Accident sites are different and the same. It is nighttime, it is morning, there are markers, there aren't, there are five miles between sites or five hundred.

Charlie's map is crisscrossed with blue; she doesn't chart a course. She's in Utah; ten days later she's in Utah again. At a truck stop in northern Louisiana she stands transfixed before a swiveling display stand of window insignias shaped like the fifty states. Now they're just ordinary stickers, but she remembers when they were decals, packaged in cellophane bags. Her mother would buy two in each state: one for the car and one for the road trip scrapbook. When immersed in water the decals would slide off their paper backing, the glue coming to life slippery and thick. She and her brother would fight over who got to apply a new one to the rear window of the station wagon.

Heather's emails wait for her at corporate coffeehouses. Charlie collects them, reads them at night on her foam mattress. *Ralph has fleas,* Heather writes. *I got a raise. I'm writing until you tell me to stop.* Charlie has always been lousy at knowing what needs to be said. Heather has seized on this communication deficiency, stubbornly establishing for them both that Charlie's silence means that the relationship isn't over.

Summer 1989, nearing sunset in northern New York State, fifty miles from the Canadian border: "You got the Tour Book back there, Charlene?" her father said. "Find us a room."

"There's a Howard Johnson's in twenty miles," Charlie told him. She was dying for a Jacuzzi, dying to find people her own age, dying to sit at the pool and drink diet soda. To make friends with an edgy girl who came from somewhere interesting.

"Howard Johnson's, pish!" Charlie's mother said. "Find us a mom and pop. Find us a Shangri-La Motor Inn. A Pink Owl Motel!"

Which is how they ended up at a renovated French Canadian chateau overlooking Lake Ontario. No Jacuzzi, no soda machine, no possibility to meet another traveling girl with whom to chatter. Just a tiny round bedroom inside a turret that her parents, with a wink to the proprietor, rented just for Charlie, where she gazed not unhappily through a skinny fortress window at the lake below, like a teenage *princesse* waiting for her life to begin.

In Mexico, Charlie waits an hour to cross the border back to Arizona. She found a white cement shrine at the site where the husband of the *turista* had been abandoned. A Virgin of Guadalupe statuette stood under an arch, protected from the sun. A plastic bag whipped in the wind, snagged on a bouquet of plastic flowers. The Polaroid developed with a bright, dusty haze. She cannot stand the feeling of exposure caused by traveling outside the Triple-A map system.

The Ruth and Geoffrey Leaf family will be in Florida any day now, wandering a narrow coastal road in their minivan, Ruth in the passenger seat frowning over her TripTik and muttering *this isn't what we asked for.* In the back seat the kids will turn away from their headrest DVD players to wonder at the synchronicity of pelicans flying low over the waves. The little girl will open her window and cup the breeze in her hand to capture the feel of flying, her wingtips kissing the water.

At a Circle K on the western edge of Tucson, Charlie buys a topographical map and finds the Globeberry Wash where it intersects Greasewood Road. The fallen saguaro has a dozen arms, some of them longer and wider than Charlie herself. She bends over the corpse of the cactus, examining. Its thin green skin is blackened and cracked; an oozing, gelatinous substance seeps from the fissures. The stench of decay is astonishing.

A pack rat scurries into a thicket of creosote. Earth is disturbed, evidence of heavy machinery having been used to move the cactus from the roadway. Her Tour Book says the State of Arizona prohibits tampering with fallen saguaros, in defense of the ecosystem that thrives inside the carcass. Another decade will pass, it tells her, before the outer casing decomposes to reveal the woody ribs beneath. Also on the page is a picture of an actual Roadrunner, which looks nothing like the cartoon.

Yosemite. New England in the fall. Manhattan for Christmas. Chesapeake Bay for the Fourth of July. The Redwoods, Four Corners, Mount Rushmore, Big Sur. Death Valley, Hollywood, Lake Michigan, the Florida Keys. Her father took them to every state in the Union connected by asphalt. He exceeded the speed limit, cared not a whit about seat belts, drove under the influence of fatigue and bickering children and sips of whiskey from a silver flask nestled between his legs. He showed them miracle after miracle.

In twenty-nine hours she arrives in Juniper Beach. A Holiday Inn Express stands where the cottages once were. The girl at the front desk tells her those old huts were infested with termites anyhow. She asks for the Ruth and Geoffrey Leaf family, but they've already checked out. Her room has a postcard view of the Atlantic Ocean and its wide, empty shoreline.

 the queer zoo

here's no actual policy at the Queer Zoo against hiring straight people; that would be illegal. Sam is alert to rumors about the existence of other hetero employees, but so far none have turned out to be true.

Sam cleans cages. Primates, birds, elephants. No, not cages: enclosures. At the Queer Zoo, the word "cage" is forbidden. Sam's girlfriend, Teri, says he underestimates his coworkers, that he ought to come out, already, that they're more open-minded than he gives them credit for. But it would be absurd, after all this time, to admit he isn't gay.

The Queer Zoo is home to the world's largest collection of homosexual, bisexual, and transgender animals. Our two-hundred-acre compound includes an African savanna, habitat to fourteen species of antelope, five giraffes, and world-famous lesbian elephants Kikora and Irene, who became famous for co-parenting Irene's baby after she was forcibly inseminated by zookeepers in San Diego. We are best known for our primates, which number more than seventy-five and include the largest collection in North America of Bonobo chimpanzees.

It's six in the morning, summer work hours. Sam is inside the Bonobo habitat. Bixby, his favorite, approaches the young male who arrived from the Bronx three weeks ago. She peers into his eyes. Ninety-eight percent of Bonobos are bisexual. But not Bixby; she doesn't like girls at all. So far the idiot primate zoologist has failed to notice. As Sam gathers the hose and shovel, Bixby's half-cousin, Tina, shoves her hand between Bixby's legs. Bixby screams in protest, then turns away from Tina and crosses her arms.

Tina has been pursuing Bixby ever since they reached adolescence. Pursuit is one of those things, Sam believes, that keeps your average people distracted from the desperation of their lives. He used to be a big fan of pursuit, of reaching. But it turns out that ridding yourself of a desire for more isn't as hard as it seems. Sam has come to accept that all he wants is to work on his screenplay, clean cages, and live with Teri. But he keeps this information to himself: if Teri understood the degree to which he is already happy with his life, with his comfort in the smallness of it, well . . . she doesn't need more fuel for her exasperation. Teri's mother is Cherokee, full-blooded. Teri has a delicately hooked nose and enormous black eyes. She has never once given him head.

For the first two years of their relationship, Teri expressed amusement that Sam remained closeted at work. Over time, her good humor waned and now she says the whole situation is just fucked up. When his co-workers come to their house, the little orange and purple cottage in the desert with its corrugated tin roof, Sam introduces her as his sister.

The operating budget of the Queer Zoo is $19.6 million. In terms of financial resources, we are the twelfth-largest zoo in the United States. The zoo attracts 500,000 visitors a year: we are among the busiest tourist attractions in Arizona, second only to the Grand Canyon. Our mission is to raise public awareness about the biological fact of homosexuality while bringing a fun and educational experience to children and families.

If it were up to Sam, the mission statement of the Queer Zoo would have better syntax.

Five years ago, Alice, the philanthropist who founded the zoo, asked Sam to fill out an application for a foundation grant to expand the antelope habitat. Until that point, all Sam had written was a series of unpublished screenplays. But the foundation gave them the money. Sam wrote another proposal and that project was funded, too. Alice offered him a promotion from enclosure custodian to grant writer but he turned it down. Sam believes that artists must conserve their creative energy by taking mundane jobs to pay the bills. Suitable work, in Sam's view, would include brewing coffee, repairing fences, or grooming poodles. But to keep Alice happy, he writes an occasional request for funding, as long as it doesn't interfere with the hosing away of animal feces. To date, his proposals have raised four million dollars for the zoo.

The Queer Zoo (formerly the Alice West Same-Sex Animal Sanctuary) grew out of the personal collection of homosexual animals gathered by Alice West. Later, Ms. West was persuaded by key members of the Arizona scientific research and tourism sectors to open her private reserve to the public. Soon thereafter, the zoo received accreditation from the American Zoological Association and acquired Zen and Len, male panda bears who had pair-bonded at the Cincinnati

Zoo and needed a home in which visitors would not be offended by their public displays of affection. Len died of natural causes three year ago. Zen has yet to pair-bond with another panda.

The primate zookeeper begins to develop suspicions about Bixby's sexuality. He asks Sam to help him set up an observation enclosure, into which he places Bixby and three other females, Tina included. Bixby slumps on her platform, pulling apart palm leaves. Two of the other females become infatuated with each other. Tina tries repeatedly to gain Bixby's sexual favors, receiving shrill, freaked-out screeches in response. The primate zookeeper scribbles on a clipboard. "Holy shit," he says, the dream of professional glory in his eyes. "The last known heterosexual Bonobo died in captivity last year."

"Maybe she's just tired," Sam suggests.

Alice shows up the next afternoon while Sam is hosing off the shovels. She's the zoo's founder and primary patron and also the executive director and president of the governing board. She hands him a manila envelope. Inside is a Request for Proposals, deadline in three days.

"Perfect for the Bixby thing." Alice takes the hose from Sam and turns the nozzle, too hard, on a dirty shovel. A spray of water and shit ricochets off the metal and splatters her sneakers.

"New Science Foundation?" Sam says. "Never heard of them."

"New funder. Big money." Alice is a practicing alcoholic. Sam suspects she's chosen a career that places her outdoors so she can wear sunglasses most of the day.

Sam scans the page. "Two hundred thousand?" He looks at Alice. "Can we spend that much?"

"Oh yeah, easy," Alice says. She tips a wheelbarrow caked with green crap on its side. "Get with what's-his-name. He's waiting to hear from you."

Sam keeps one eye on Alice and reads the RFP. Sam has been employed at the Queer Zoo longer than anyone else on staff. Alice hired him when he was in college to help her care for what was then just a personal menagerie. This was before there was a board of directors, a human resources manual. Despite everything, despite her drinking, despite the peculiar way she's chosen to dispense of her fortune, despite the ongoing low hum of discontent among his coworkers about her autocratic leadership, Sam has never been able to dislike Alice. She does her best, and she loves the animals.

She gives the wheelbarrow a thorough cleaning. "Thanks," Sam says.

"Least I can do," Alice replies.

At dinner that night, Teri invents a plan to rescue Bixby from her fate as a laboratory curiosity. She'll sabotage the research, she says, by releasing pheromones into the Bonobo habitat, confusing the chimps into irregular sexual behaviors.

Sam points out that the Queer Zoo's security system is state-of-the-art, designed to dissuade religious fundamentalists. Besides, chimpanzee pheromones can't be all that easy to find.

Teri snorts and scrapes her chair away from the table. It is a thrift-store chair upon which she has shellacked images of Frida Kahlo paintings. In her New York years, Teri and a band of radical feminists did "direct action": they poured red dye into the fountain at Columbus Circle to represent the blood to be spilled if abortion were made illegal; crashed presidential fund-raising dinners to yell about AIDS in Africa; chained themselves to a cosmetics counter at Macy's in protest of animal testing. Now she's a ranger at Kartchner Caverns State Park in Benson. She spends hours of each day in the cool underground, leading tourists around in the dark.

Two years ago, a heterosexual female Bonobo was born at the Queer Zoo. Despite sustained observation, she has never been seen engag-

ing in same-sex behavior, nor does she exhibit any of the strongly female-identified bonding behaviors universal to her sex. She is a rare discovery indeed. While scores of studies have been published on the homosexual and bisexual behaviors of the Bonobo chimpanzee, none have been performed on those 2 percent that have exhibited consistent and stubborn opposite-sex behavior. A suspected heterosexual female is part of the collection at the Beijing Zoo, however, zookeepers appear uninterested in pursuing a scientific study of her case. Unknown others are surely in captivity all over the world.

Sam's screenplay is about a middle-aged guy who works at a zoo. The protagonist falls in love with a homeless woman who spends her days in the aviary. Every day she sits for hours on a bench dedicated to the memory of her brother. It's a story about the redemption to be found in love. Sam has been writing the manuscript for eight years. Teri has stopped asking whether he'll ever show it to her.

He sits at his computer at the tiny desk in the living room. Teri has had this desk since she was in junior high school. Last year she dragged it out of the attic in her mother's house and refinished it as Mexican folk art shabby chic but left pasted on the inside of the top drawer the photo of Ani DiFranco she'd glued there as a teenager.

He attempts to revise the second scene of Act Three. He's having difficulty getting his protagonist, Jerry, to tell the homeless woman he's in love with her. Among his strategies for Jerry's characterization is to give the guy a manner of speaking that is clipped and controlled. Basically, Jerry doesn't say much, a trait that causes problems on many levels throughout the screenplay. Recently Sam tried to work on the script after having smoked an inordinate amount of weed. In the light of day it all turned out to be crap.

As he writes, Teri is on the couch with her face behind *Biological Exuberance: Third Edition*, the seven-hundred-page bible of the queer zoology field. The house is warm; it's monsoon season and the swamp coolers can't handle the humidity. She wears a sports bra and stretch shorts. "It says here"—Sam notices she's reading the tiny print of the endnotes—"that scientists trying to determine whether female rhesus monkeys experienced orgasm strapped them to an apparatus made of iron and wood and forced them to undergo stimulation with a dildo." She puts the book down and stares at Sam openmouthed, as if he were the one responsible for securing the money that funded this particular atrocity.

"That study happened something like fifty years ago," he says.

"And here's another one," she says. "A gender-mixing Savanna Baboon in South Africa was shot and dissected to 'study' its reproductive organs." She frames the word "study" in air quotes. "Another was captured and given hormone treatments," she screeches, "to see if it would behave like a normal female!"

"Those research methods were discredited before either of us were born," Sam tells her.

Teri sighs, that put-upon sigh that signals a wide range of dissatisfactions. "Villainy!" she says. She jumps to her feet and places one hand on her hips, shakes the book at him. "Rape and murder!" She's just been at the gym. She smells enticingly of sweat. The sweat of neck and forehead and of the hollow between the breasts and also a midsummer pussy sweat.

"Tell me they aren't going to hurt that monkey," Teri says. She grins at the effect her body is having on him.

"Chimpanzee, actually."

"Sam! Tell me they aren't going to poke her with needles or strap her to a chair or harass her with electronics." She's all elbows and raised eyebrows and wild hair. "Or rape her!"

"They're ethical people. Plus if they did anything out of bounds they'd lose accreditation."

"Out of bounds? What's in bounds? What's lawful? Is autopsy lawful?"

"Under certain circumstances, but they've never—"

"Tell Alice you won't do it," Teri says. "Otherwise you'll be entirely, wholly, karmically to blame." With each adverb she pushes her finger into his chest.

A summer monsoon begins its thrum on their tin roof. They turn toward the window. "Enough already," Sam says.

Teri leans in to kiss him. "Just say you won't do it, baby. I got your back," she whispers into his mouth.

Scientists at the Alice West Animal Sexuality Research Institute believe that the location and structure of the female Bonobo's genitals—a large clitoris that swells to nearly double its regular size during sexual arousal—has evolved uniquely for the purpose of lesbian genitor-genital (GG) rubbing. Comparable physical evolution is not found in the male Bonobo. Females often have many sexual partners, with group activity not uncommon. An average of two-thirds of all female Bonobo sexual interactions are homosexual, and females participate in GG rubbing on average every 2.3 hours. It is typical of the female Bonobo to develop strong bonds and lasting relationships not only for sexual activity but also for grooming, playing, and the formation of social alliances.

On his lunch break, Sam wanders over to the accounting office to see if his friend Brian has eaten yet. But he's already gone, probably to meet his partner Dave for a picnic by the ground squirrels. Sam leaves a note on his monitor. *Drop by the house tonight to visit Mary Jane.* This is as much obliqueness as he can muster regarding their weed habit. He sighs at the note. *Bring Dave*, he adds lamely.

Brian and his lover Dave raise the cannabis in their greenhouse alongside their blue-ribbon orchids. Dave manages the zoo's gift shop. Brian began growing when Dave underwent chemo for testicular cancer. When the cancer was gone, Brian and Dave just kept on. They'd developed the habit, Brian says. Dave lost both balls. Which, Sam figures, makes him entitled to all the weed he wants. Brian and Dave, like everyone else at work, are ignorant about his heterosexual love for Teri. Sam doesn't like keeping this information from them, given that they're the closest human friends he has at work. Not that they'd reject him. After the cancer, they mellowed out considerably on the question of queer politics; their conversation these days is littered with references to The Big Picture. So his deception is pointless and stupid. It's a small thing that's become huge, like informing your wife she has horrible breath.

Before he leaves for the day, Sam drops by to check on Bixby. She dozes on a branch in a pen the size of a tool shed, twitching in her sleep. He wonders if she dreams about Mr. Bronx, or about her mother, maybe, or about the primate zookeeper and his clipboard. At home he figures he should get some writing done before Brian and Dave come over. He tries to read the script as if he's someone else, seeing the language for the first time. He pretends to believe in its beauty. All Jerry needs is to get the hell over himself. Tough love is what Jerry needs.

He's so deep into the work that when Brian and Dave show up he wonders why they've come. He has written ten pages of a new scene, and much of it could be worth keeping. They sit on the back patio in his aluminum chairs, smoking and gazing at the darkening sky. The sunset is pretty much dead.

"Mars is really close right now," Dave says. He points to the east.

"That's an airplane, sweetie," Brian says.

They laugh unrestrainedly for a while. Nothing really matters, Sam thinks happily. He's grateful for his friends, and he knows now that whatever problems he has with his manuscript and with Teri and Alice are inconsequential. Bixby will be fine. The primate zoologist is a good person, devoted to the animals.

When Teri comes home they're all in the kitchen, investigating the contents of the refrigerator. "Hi, Sis!" Sam says. She is beautiful, standing there in her ranger uniform, the pants ill fitting but somehow sexy, gazing in disapproval at the three toasted and sheepish men in her kitchen.

It occurs to Sam that this could be the moment in which Teri is deciding she's finally had enough of his directionless existence, of his paranoid deception about their coupledom, of his failure to stand up for Bixby, of his inability to occupy an identity as a writer. With regard to women, he realizes, he lives just on the edge of fear. Take Alice, take Teri. Is there any way to not feel unsettled by them?

A grand and important gesture is what's called for, right here and now. He'll tell her he loves her, he'll sweep her into his arms in front of Brian and Dave, plant a non-sibling-like kiss on her extraordinary Cherokee lips. He takes a step toward Teri, to embrace her with all the biological exuberance in his heart, but she's already turned her back.

It is our pleasure to present to the New Science Foundation this proposal for $200,000. With your support and under the direction of the Queer Zoo's chief primate zookeeper, a team of animal behavioralists and zoologists at the Alice West Animal Sexuality Research Institute will perform a comprehensive study of the Bonobo female in an effort to discover the reasons for her heterosexuality. She will undergo a series of tests to analyze her behavior with Bonobos of both sexes, including sustained placement with small groups made up exclusively of males and of females.

When Sam comes home from work the next evening, he finds Teri lying on her back on their couch, reading his script. "Hey!" he shouts, ready to snatch it from her. She puts one palm toward him in a stop-right-there-buddy gesture, and he does.

"This is ridiculous, Sam," she says from behind the mask of manuscript.

"It's not ready," he whines. "It's a work in progress, you shouldn't—"

"I mean it's silly that I haven't seen this. After all this time." She lowers the manuscript and he sees she's been crying. She's cried twice before, in his presence. Once when her grandfather died and once when she dropped a gallon jar of pickles on her foot, breaking three tiny bones.

"What?" he says. "Baby, what?"

"What do you think, dope? This shit is beautiful."

The skin under Sam's hair tingles electrically. "You think?"

She raises the pages in front of her face again. She's a body lying on the couch: breasts, stomach, bare legs, his script for a head. "I'm almost done. Make us some dinner, huh?"

The physiology of our heterosexual Bonobo female will be studied to determine the existence of any deformities of sexual organs and/or hormonal imbalances, such as an abundance of progesterone. Scientists will conduct an endocrinologic analysis and ovarian ultrasound measurement to uncover the possibility of an unusual hormonal profile. The study will include blood tests to look for possible microorganisms or contaminants, an analysis of her diet, a study of her chromosomes, and an ovarian biopsy. Her environment will also be examined for possible soil toxins and air pollutants to determine whether she might suffer from primate chemical sensitivity syndrome.

At work, Sam spends nearly an hour looking for Alice. Her assistant says she's out on the savanna with the lions; the penguin zookeeper says she's in a sales meeting. He chases a trail of employee hearsay and at last finds her coming out of the women's bathroom near the snack bar. "Have you read my first draft?" he asks.

"Let's sit," she says. They sidle into plastic chairs, attached to a plastic table. A fine coat of moisture covers its surface from the cooling water misters attached to the faux ocotillo ceiling of the picnic ramada overhead. Alice pulls his draft out of the back pocket of her Wranglers and unfolds it. She flips through the document. "Primate chemical sensitivity syndrome?" She looks up from the page. "That's a thing?"

"Apparently."

Shaking her head, she runs her finger along Sam's pages, stopping at the end of the paragraph. She snorts a laugh. "'Uncovering the source of her aberrant monosexuality'? You came up with this?"

Sam shrugs modestly.

"Invasive procedures, up to and including surgery, will be performed only when all other methods have proven inconclusive," she reads, making a face. "This comes from what's-his-name?"

"Conforms to best practices, he said."

"Best practices." Alice removes her glasses and stares over Sam's head, at the mountains beyond the zoo. She chews a mint, which doesn't do much to address the smell of the vodka seeping from her pores. "Our guys won't cut her open," she says.

Last night, postcoitally, Teri told Sam a story as penance for having taken his script. She whispered a tale about her grandfather, Ata'-gul kalu', commonly translated as Leaning Wood, who in 1988 stood for seven days at the entrance to a sacred canyon, blocking a bulldozer sent with the blessing of the Oklahoma legislature to clear forty acres of ancestral burial ground for a new highway connecting the city of Tulsa to a pristine patch of wilderness central to the long-range business plan of U.S. Homes, Incorporated. Leaning Wood didn't sleep for a week. He peed where he stood and stole off behind a boulder to defecate in the predawn hours while the bulldozer driver, ordered by the suits at HQ to stand firm, slept in the cab. Teri told him, sweaty from sex, lips at his neck, damp sheet twisted around her legs, fingers playing absently with his pubic hair, that Leaning Wood didn't have a lawyer or a publicist or a support team. All he had was a backpack full of water and venison jerky, a pair of comfortable hiking boots and the collected works of Henry David Thoreau.

When she was done Sam said, "I wrote the proposal."

Her body went heavy against his. "Oh, babe," she said. "Oh, fuck."

Now Sam says, "Alice." Her head is down, frowning at his prose. "I don't know. Maybe let's draw a line with this one. So that next time . . ."

"Slippery slope?" Alice says. "Too late. We're already halfway down that hill. The otter project last year, the penguins before that. I can't subsidize the zoo forever." Alice pulls out a pen, signs the cover letter. "Why the hell am I explaining myself?" she mutters.

Tonya, the new antelope zookeeper with the beautiful ass and terrifically tanned legs, jogs past their table and waves. "That springbok is in labor!" she says.

"Radio me when she's close!" Alice shouts. Births are a relative rarity at the zoo, given their policy against forced insemination. Alice watches Tonya until she's rounded the bend beyond the toucan habitat. To distract Alice from his own careful study of Tonya's ass, he raises her eyebrows at her in accusation. Alice has a thing for younger women.

"Don't start with me. She's straight," Alice says. "Boyfriend's big as a mountain."

Sam cannot manage a response to the news of another heterosexual on the grounds. "Maybe we'll get rejected," he tells her.

"No, we'll get it," Alice says. "The president of the foundation is an old friend. Do you realize how a study on bisexuality could change the whole conversation? What if sexuality *is* a choice? So goddamn what?" She regards him emptily. "Just send it in."

Teri arrives home after midnight and gets into bed ungently, shaking the mattress.

"No use pretending you're asleep," she says into the darkness. She's lying on her back. Her profile is just visible, an obstinate shadow.

"I just want to keep my job," he tells her.

She sits up in the bed accusingly. "Did you mail the proposal?"

"It's my job, Teri," he says.

"Have you ever asked me, Sam, if I'm straight?"

He props himself up on an elbow. "Are you?"

She lays her head on the pillow. "I have to get up early."

He used to think, in the early years, that when she left the room or closed her eyes he was supposed to drop the subject, let the argument go. He has since come to recognize this trap: she only looks like she's done talking.

"I'm not like you," he says. In the semidarkness he stares at the brown patches on the ceiling where the roof leaked last summer. "I'm bad with confrontation." There is actually no way to win an argument with Teri; there are only degrees of losing.

"I thought we were sleeping now," she says.

"I thought we were working something out," he says back. That's good, he thinks. The reason he's always losing these things is a simple failure to play offense.

Teri puts her hands over her eyes. "Let me tell you something, Sam," she says.

Still, here, even after the hands over her eyes, even after the intake of breath, even after the pause she takes to choose her best words, he clings brightly to the notion that this moment might resolve in his favor.

The swamp cooler emits its nocturnal clunks. Outside: rodents and crickets.

"Here's the thing," she says, dooming him. "I'm not angry. I'm resigned. And you know what? I've made some choices that put me at blame, too. It's not your fault, babe. You are who you are. You're never going to do anything with your screenplay. You're this great guy, this real sweetheart, and that's it. But you know, that's just fine. It's fine."

"Charlie Kaufman worked on *Being John Malkovich* for nearly twenty years," he says, having no idea if it's true.

"I've got to decide, is all," she continues. "Can I live with this? At this point it has so little to do with you."

"Well treat me like a kid, why don't you?"

"It's not my job to take care of your feelings," she says.

"What have you been reading?"

"Go to sleep now," she tells him.

"Are you trying to tell me you're not straight?"

But she isn't kidding. She really is done. Sam watches the rise and fall of her back, willing her to turn over and harangue him some more.

The Queer Zoo enjoys a stellar reputation among zoologists, animal-rights activists, the LGBT community, and the general public. Year after year, our inhabitants score at least ten percentage points higher on independent evaluative physical exams than the national average for animals in captivity. From our spacious habitats—considered among the most humane in the Western hemisphere—to our clean and comfortable research facilities, the Queer Zoo is above all preoccupied with ensuring the health and happiness of the animals in our care.

Teri isn't in their bed the next morning. When Sam arrives at work, she's standing outside the entrance to the zoo with a handmade sign that says SAVE BIXBY.

"What are you doing?"

"Saving Bixby's life!" she says. Her sole audience at this hour of the morning is a pair of women and five staring kids, lingering in confusion at the ticket window.

He points to the windows of the zoo's administration office. "You'll get me fired."

"It's not my job to look after your paycheck," Teri says. She's redfaced, neck blotchy and strained. "It's not my job to ask you to show up."

"Show up where?" Sam says.

On the cafeteria television, Sam and a dozen coworkers watch the news at noon, broadcast live from their parking lot. Teri delivers her soundbites to a TV reporter. Below her image, the screen reads "Friend of Bixby."

When the broadcast is over, Sam stands outside the cafeteria, pondering the best enclosure in which to lay low. Alice appears, the broken blood vessels on her cheeks in a state of pink agitation. She's been looking for him. "You told your wingnut sister about Bixby?"

"I didn't think she'd—"

"Did you mail the proposal?" Alice says. There is a grease spot on her blouse. Sam can't seem to look away from it. "Did you?"

"Went out yesterday," Sam says.

He watches her deciding whether to believe him. "From now on, let's just have you focus on cleaning cages," she finally says.

"Enclosures," he tells her.

"Get your girlfriend out of our parking lot, Sam. Or else you can just go on home."

"Sister," Sam says.

Alice turns her back and walks across the main plaza, past the information booth. She stoops to pick up a crumpled napkin.

He finds Brian and Dave in the cafeteria. "Will you guys do me a favor?"

"Teri's doing quite a job out there," Brian says.

"She's not my sister," Sam says. "I'm not gay."

Brian and Dave blink, nearly in unison. "Sam," Brian says. "Sammy. This is not news." He lays his hand on Sam's cheek.

"I'll tell you what," Dave says. "I think Teri is right about Bixby."

"It's kind of a big favor," Sam says.

"Will we be implicated in any wrongdoing?" Brian asks him. "I've always wanted to be implicated."

Bixby is docile in Sam's arms. He holds her on his hip like a baby. When they leave the observation cage, Cousin Tina shrieks at them. Hot air settles on his skin. On the main promenade, children point. He passes the gift shop, where through the window he sees Brian and Dave in earnest conversation with the security guard. She's writing soberly on her pad. When Sam left them, they were plotting a story about a band of androgynous teenage shoplifters.

Out in the parking lot, a thousand invisible cicadas shriek at the blazing sun. Bixby's fingers grip his neck. The saguaro cacti on the distant foothills resemble an army of furry toothpicks. At the sight of the chimp, Teri lets out a yip of joy. Bixby responds, a shrill scream in his ear, and clambers onto his shoulders.

Together they run across the expanse of parking lot to his car, in the employee section at the northern end. He starts the engine. "My god, babe," Teri says, grinning in fear. "What have we done?"

"Get out," he says, winded.

"What?" she says. "What do you mean?"

"Get out of the car. Tell them the truth. Tell them you had no idea." The steering wheel burns his palms like an invitation to adventure. He kisses Teri goodbye. She leaves the car, bewildered and beautiful.

Bixby settles in the passenger seat and looks expectantly out of the windshield. How easy it is, Sam thinks, just to let go.

housework

anny and Betsy have settled on "nesting," a system of divorce espoused by certain how-to books in which the children stay in the family home and the parents take turns vacating it. Betsy and Danny agree on practically nothing, yet have managed to come together on the subject of minimizing the kids' suffering.

Normally, nesting requires three domiciles: the home currently occupied by the kids and their Parent of the Week, one for the husband, and one for the wife. Betsy and Danny can't afford a mortgage plus two rents, so they've leased a single studio apartment only large enough for one person. The parent who isn't at home with Jason and Meghan, who isn't carrying on as if everything were normal and fine, finds him- or herself holed up in the room with the brown carpet and the brown cabinets and the brown interior doors.

They've become roommates; the kind that never see one another.

When Danny isn't being a father he's slouched on the rented sleeper sofa in this stucco dungeon, wearing down the buttons on the remote. When Betsy isn't being a mother she's curled on the sofa bed's thin mattress, sleeping, eating, or crying. Or she's having sex with one of the two men she's dating. Each of these men wants more from her than she's willing to give.

When Betsy comes into the apartment after her week with the kids, she feels the residue of Danny's grief rising up from the stale carpet. By choosing a place with the décor of depression and an absence of natural light, they've managed simultaneously to punish both themselves and each other.

Betsy and Danny are tidy people. Except for their toiletries, which they each have purchased in duplicate, they leave nothing in the apartment. It is as impersonal as a hotel room. In unspoken agreement they both erase any trace of themselves before they leave. They wash their dishes and dry them and put them away in the cupboards. When Danny moved into the studio, he brought the cups and plates they'd packed away and put in the shed four years ago. These are the same dishes they ate from when they first moved in together, when they were young.

Over the years, Danny and Betsy have developed identical domestic habits. When Danny comes back from the kids' house, the kitchen in the studio apartment is so clean that he cannot tell whether Betsy has cooked anything at all in the past week. Technically, it was he who left the marriage. Thanks to his lawyer, he has come to learn about the legal difference between being the one left in a house versus being the one who puts some stuff in a bag and goes away.

Nesting, Danny has learned, is what emotionally advanced people do when they divorce. Adults of the new millennium, adults of divorced parents, adults like him and like Betsy, remember the acrimony interwoven into childhoods spent in two households.

In the home that has now become known as the kids' house, Danny leaves no sign of his struggle with single parenthood. For a host of complicated reasons, including the preservation of his dignity; his ongoing fears about future custody; and his need to demonstrate to Betsy she's not, after all, the critical presence around the house he'd always amiably agreed she was, Danny will not leave undone housework in his wake. The laundry hamper becomes the bellwether of his domestic competence. He establishes an imaginary line in its faux wicker weave, roughly one-third from the bottom. The level of kids' dirty clothes must never top this line. He cannot have Betsy coming here after her days in studio apartment exile to any evidence that he's falling apart.

Betsy buys Windex at the drugstore and cleans all the windows in the studio apartment. She uses a toothbrush and a diluted bleach mixture to whiten the grout around the tiles in the shower stall. She rents a steam cleaner and runs it repeatedly over the carpet, emptying bucketsful of thick gray water from the machine. One of the guys she's sleeping with calls and asks her to dinner. She wipes her forehead with the back of her grimy wrist and tells him she's busy.

Danny is not unfamiliar with where things belong in the kids' house, how things should be kept. He knows where the cleansers are stored, which kind is to be used on the bathtub and which on the linoleum. When the kids were newborns he took paternity leave. He cooked and cleaned while Betsy napped or nursed. He waited on her; made sure she got what she needed for breastfeeding. Got out of bed to fetch the infant when it cried in the middle of the night. When people came to the house to see the new baby, Betsy would refer to him as her domestic partner. Still, Danny cultivated a tolerance for disorder; a quality of agreeableness about human-made messes he believed was necessary to be the type of parent he wanted to be: relaxed, understanding. Since the nesting experiment, this quality has evaporated. The kids frown at his personality change, their tender brows furrowed in disapproval. They watch him scrub the counter-tops, vacuum the carpet. After a few weeks, they adapt. He observes their little minds gravely accepting the news that their reality now includes an additional parent overly concerned about dirt.

In the studio apartment, Betsy examines the food on Danny's side of the refrigerator. Beer, soy milk, olives, cheese. It is the food of their marriage. She does not eat any of it, ever. Likewise, Danny has never touched any of her food, never borrowed anything. She would know: with her fingernail or a pencil she leaves nearly imperceptible marks on the labels to indicate the quantities remaining. The refrigerator at the kids' house is a different matter. Tubes of yogurt, pudding cups, single-serve applesauces.

One of the guys Betsy is dating is a carpenter of sorts, employed more often than he isn't. He takes her to a cowboy bar at the edge of town where they drink beers and he teaches her to two-step across the sawdust floor. He is wiry, more muscular than Danny but less physically solid. She met him when her girlfriends took her out drinking in one of those women-only rituals designed to celebrate the lousiness of marriage and the marvelous freedom of single womanhood but which are inevitably infused with a pathetic false hilarity. A sympathetic grin and a single Jack Daniels, neat, and she'd been in the front seat of the carpenter's Ford pickup, waving goodbye to the strained smiles of her middle-aged posse.

Danny's coworker sets him up with her sister. They go on a date characterized primarily by politeness. The coworker's sister is attractive in the resigned way some beautiful women are, warm on the surface and wary immediately below. They go to a restaurant, a place Danny had checked out the week before and found charming but which she informed him, upon arrival, was a franchise out of California. She reveals small bits of information about herself, doling out personal statements in pieces, waiting for his own as if in trade for hers. It does not occur to him, until he's back at the studio apartment, to compare her to Betsy. He takes this as a promising sign.

He and Betsy were together, more or less amiably, for nine years before the kids. They met at Betsy's high school prom; he'd been the date of someone's cousin, a girl who attended Betsy's school. She went with a bunch of other girls, a jaded pack without boyfriends. Over the head of his date he watched her dance, attracted by her loose, arm-jangling absence of self-consciousness. She didn't want kids. She would only screw them up, she'd said, and whether or not he knew it, so would he. On the couch in the dark studio apartment he now wonders whether he'd have pushed her to get pregnant even if he knew the kids would mean the end of their marriage. It's a ridiculous question. He stares at the sparkly texturing crap adhered to the ceiling and tries to tell himself that the kids are sufficient tradeoff for all of this.

The other guy Betsy's dating is what they call a bodyworker. He gives backrubs, in other words, to vacationers at the resort hotels in the foot-hills. He has a nose that dominates his face but the way he uses his hands is magnificent, a real advantage. He likes to talk. In this way he's more woman than man: he likes to talk not just about himself, as most men-talkers do, but about her as well. He likes to listen to her, to ask her questions about herself and her feelings. She's annoyed by this behavior and has lately been asking herself if his hands are worth it. She knows he's working his way into asking about Danny, about the kids, about what went wrong, about why she refuses to convert the couch into a bed when they have sex, why they can't do it between the sheets.

Now they have three checking accounts. One for Danny, one for Betsy, and one for the kids. The mortgage is paid from the kids' account, as are their shoes and clothing, music lessons, the minivan payment. There is currently an excess of three thousand dollars in the kids' account, a fact

Betsy, who manages the money, has not shared with Danny. She has never been particularly frugal: although she believes in the merit of keeping an emergency reserve, she's more likely to fold to the temptation of purchasing a new swing set, a digital camera.

Danny and Betsy have agreed to perform their parental switches after the children are asleep, to eliminate the strain on the kids of seeing their estranged parents in the same room and to reduce the possibility they will harbor hopes of reconciliation. Meghan and Jason, on Danny's Monday mornings, have developed the habit of rushing into the bedroom and jumping him awake as a means of welcoming him home after his week away. He suspects, although he does not ask, that they have the same ritual with their mother. Routine, he reminds himself, is one of the most important elements of a healthy childhood.

Betsy continues to refer to the situation as "our separation." Danny calls it "our circumstances." Their civility, he thinks, is perhaps more disturbing than anything.

On Sunday nights at the kids' house, Danny is always ready to go when Betsy pulls up. He meets her outside in the driveway.

"Hey," she says. She hands him the keys to his truck.

"Couldn't get Meghan in the bath tonight," Danny says.

"Right," Betsy says. She carries her suitcase by its handle, even though she could just as easily wheel it into the house. She looks tired. Or is it something else? Some newly developed state of her being?

"What else?" she says.

"Some girl bit Jason in school yesterday."

"Carolina?" Betsy says. "She likes him."

"Hardly broke the skin," Danny says.

She brushes past him, up the walk. "Soccer is at four next weekend," he says to her back.

"Got it," she says. She turns to look at him. "That it?"

"Okay," he says. "Yeah."

She goes through the door and closes it behind her. He forgot to tell her they're almost out of milk.

Back at the studio apartment, a pair of Betsy's pants is hanging in the closet. A dirty spoon sits at the bottom of the kitchen sink. He examines the evidence, the lines of yogurt residue left by the movement of the spoon through her lips. He places it, unwashed, on the shelf next to the microwave.

Danny watches a lot of television. He sees an advertisement for a family cruise vacation that touts onboard opportunities for "togethering." It's simple, he reminds himself: Betsy is the kind of person who needs time alone. So much time that she shouldn't have had children. She is not a lousy parent, but rather the kind for whom it is difficult to make the necessary sacrifices. She has a low threshold for the physical closeness and unrelenting, innocent demands of children. Danny has never been able to understand Betsy's need to bring intellectual resources to the job of mothering, her tendency to gather a mountain of knowledge from books and workshops and videotapes. A quantity enough, when confronted with another of the kids' ceaseless needs, to defeat her instinct to dash into the bathroom and lock the door. She calls them her "buckets of want." She insists Danny should admire her resolve and willpower. Her cynicism, she's told him, is at least the kind that's kept among adults. She does not refer to them, within their earshot, as Those Rotten Kids, as her mother did. She does not let it spill over onto them. Danny believes it is only a matter of time before it does. He is convinced that what Betsy needs are entire weeks at a stretch without the children. In the gloom of the apartment, he broods over the impact of his absence on her parenting. He imagines her running out the front door, looking for a random stranger to absorb her narcissistic agony.

In the morning, he goes to the home improvement superstore and buys two gallons of paint. The shade is somewhere between lemon and lime. He buys another quart, in taupe, for the doors and trim. He has no opinion about this color combination, about its relative beauty or ugliness, but makes his choice based on the blessing of Martha Stewart. He also picks up some primer for the brown doors. Betsy will be pleased at what he's done, which means he hates himself for doing it. For choosing these paints, for opening the cans, for covering the rollers and brushes with it, and for applying two careful coats on the walls and four coats on each of the brown doors. He spends the afternoon in the fumes of self-disappointment.

To keep the cool air inside he hasn't opened the windows. He reclines on the pullout couch, which he's covered with a sheet of plastic. He falls asleep in his clothes, breathing a paint-fume headache into his lungs. He wakes up at three o'clock in the morning, his cheek sweating against the plastic. The overhead light puts out roughly a million watts, directly into his eyes. The paintbrush has stiffened in the pan.

In the morning, he moves the furniture back into place and discovers, between the couch cushions, a man's watch. The back is inscribed. *To my grandson; on the occasion of his high school graduation, May 1984.* He opens the window for some air. If an engraver had used that kind of lousy punctuation on his own watch, he'd have made him do it over. Danny graduated in 1982. He puts the watch in his pocket. For the rest of the week he rubs at it. He thinks about Betsy fucking a sophomore.

When he leaves the apartment, he returns the yogurt spoon to the bottom of the empty sink. Also he drops a wet towel on the bathroom floor: a terrycloth message. When Betsy arrives, he thinks, it will still be damp. She will stand over it, pondering.

Betsy has resolved to spend her week under the covers. She's planned a sort of vacation around it. She stops at the grocery store and fills the cart with food that can be microwaved or eaten directly out of the box. At the apartment she dresses in flannel pajama bottoms and a tank top, turns the air conditioning down to sixty-eight degrees. She unfolds the sofa bed and switches on the television. In the morning, she calls in sick to work. She is sick, anyway, she really is. Sick of it all. She hangs up the phone and stares at the walls and realizes they're a different color. This revelation prevents her from lying in bed, which is annoying. The new colors aren't what she needs; they refuse to shelter the seeds of her depression. She'd been relying on the brown doors to help keep her down.

She walks to the grocery store and buys a spray can of oven cleaner and a package of scrubber sponges. She empties the refrigerator, removes the wire shelves, and washes down the inside with hot, soapy water. It was a brand new fridge when they moved in, a cheap one, and after eight months she and Danny haven't gotten it the least bit dirty. The oven, also, is more or less clean, but she dives in headfirst and scrubs the hell out of the inside. The fumes from oven cleaner will probably cause some kind of long-term damage like Parkinson's disease or brain cancer. Sometimes she works herself into tears, lying in bed at night, over the possibility of childhood leukemia. Or sexual predators. Boating accidents. All along she's been obsessing over the wrong kinds of injuries. Much of the time she wishes she could sit them down, her kids, and ask them whether she's doing any sort of decent job as a parent. If only she could find a way to phrase the question so as not scare them witless. She knew, before she became a mother, that she'd fuck things up. She should have listened to herself. She let Danny wear her down. Now it's too late: she's in love with his children.

The cowboy calls. He's lost his wristwatch. It's clear he doesn't want to talk, but he chitchats for a respectable amount of time before he hangs up. She tells him she hasn't seen his watch. He fails to ask when they'll get together again. On her way out the door to the kids' house on Sunday night, Betsy leaves a pair of white socks, worn but only mildly dirty, on the coffee table. She doesn't wash the sheets on the sofa bed.

Danny waits for Betsy on the front porch of the kids' house. Since their situation began they haven't been in the house at the same time together. Danny wonders if she is even aware of this fact, whether she has guessed that the need to meet her outside has become a sort of superstition for him.

"The minivan needs an oil change," he says. "I couldn't get to it this week." Betsy nods. She looks like she's lost seven or eight pounds.

"The health insurance bill is going up," she says. "We should think about a new company." She's wearing a new pair of jeans, the kind that fit low around the hips. She's holding her suitcase but not moving toward the house.

Danny knows he should leave now. He should be the one, for a change, that cuts short the dialogue with the movement of his body, walking off as if he has somewhere else to be. "Jason has a science experiment going on the kitchen windowsill," he says. "Just to warn you."

"A school thing, or strictly recreation?" she says.

"Just for fun. Mold and such," he says. "You might want to throw away the Tupperware it's in."

"Maybe I'll let him keep it going for another week," she says. "Until he's your problem again."

The neighbor's car pulls out of their driveway and glides past them. Danny waves.

"I meant *it*," Betsy says. "Until *it's* your problem, not him."

"I knew what you meant," Danny says. It occurs to him that all along, she was clear about not wanting kids. At what point in his boyhood did he build into his worldview the idea that women who claim they don't want children are lying? How did this myth become an ingredient in the mortar of his belief system? He manipulated her; he sacrificed her to his need for fatherhood. He doesn't deserve to be forgiven.

Danny goes on another date with his coworker's sister. When he called her and asked, he was surprised she said yes. After the movie, he takes her back to the studio apartment. He has changed the sheets and moved Betsy's socks onto the shelf in the closet. Even with the new paint the place looks like a rental furniture showroom.

"Cheerful," his date says.

"Transition," Danny says. "Everything's temporary, right?" He's going for upbeat, lighthearted, a modern pseudo-Buddhist guy who takes casual sex in stride. Instead it emerges from his mouth as something Eeyore would say.

They make vigorous love, energetic, lacking creativity or humor. Danny is satisfied, though, and tender with her afterward. She isn't the first woman he's been with since his circumstances occurred. They talk for a while and drink Irish whiskey in bed. Finally she mentions her babysitter and then gets dressed. Danny walks her to the parking lot and kisses her on the nose. That's that, he thinks. Pleasant enough. Pretty.

Danny puts the unwashed sheets back on the sofa bed. The next morning he scours the kitchen linoleum. At the end of the week he places Betsy's dirty socks on the coffee table and leaves an open jar of olives, the last one still floating in brine, next to the lamp on the end table. Also he spills a small amount of cigarette ash on the carpet.

Betsy goes away for a weekend with the bodyworker. She takes the kids to her mother's house. Her mother has been complaining anyway that she doesn't see them enough. The bodyworker brings her to a ski resort owned by the same hotel chain he works for. With his employee discount he can get a room for practically nothing in the offseason. They take the ski lift to the top of the mountain and have a picnic of Brie and apples and wine and bread. The air is cool and the sun is warm and the body-worker asks Betsy to take off her clothes and let him fuck her on the grass. This is exactly how he says it. Betsy appreciates direct language of this kind—clearly he has been sensing her impatience with his sensitive guy baloney—so as a reward she acquiesces. She hasn't had sex outdoors in years.

"That was absolutely pleasant," she says afterward. They lay side-by-side on their backs, the sun warming their tender parts. In profile, the bodyworker's nose could be a foothill of the mountain range to the north.

He gives her thigh a little slap. "Absolutely," he says.

On the way home there is construction on the mountain road, and she is late picking up the kids from her mother's. When they pull up at the kids' house in the minivan, Danny is outside, sitting on the tailgate of his truck. The kids squeal at the sight of him.

"They're high on cupcakes," Betsy tells him.

"I'll put them to bed," he says. He eyes Betsy's suitcase. "Did you go somewhere?"

Jason stands between them, gazing from one parent to the other. "We went to grandma's house for the whole entire weekend, Daddy," he says.

"Her cat is dead," Megan says.

"She put M&M's in the pancakes," Jason says. "And Frosted Flakes."

Betsy puts her suitcase in the bed of the truck. "Sorry we're late," she says. He's been worrying, she can tell. Had she been a more enthusiastic mother, had she been able to cultivate the ability to put herself last, always last, as any mother with the vaguest notion of appropriate parenting should do, her relationship would be currently intact. Although she would love to blame Danny—and some days she succeeds in doing so—for his relentless wheedling, over the first four years of their marriage, in favor of procreation, she now knows the failure is ultimately hers. The truth, as it seems to be emerging, the kernel of their problem, nestled inside layer upon layer of issues related to parenting, to sacrifice, to individual desires, is this: she is, and always has been, fundamentally selfish.

When they're getting into their pajamas, Danny asks the kids about Betsy's whereabouts over the weekend. This is the kind of behavior that divorcing parents should avoid at all costs. He knows this. He can see in their faces a flicker of conflict. The children are considering the moral gray area into which they're being dragged. Which must be vastly confusing, given their preschool devotion to the concepts of right and wrong, good and bad. To tattle or not to tattle. Danny is disgusted with himself. His father was a volatile drunkard, a sloppy, selfish human who went through life deadening the spirits of the people he loved, showing up sporadically for his visitation weekends. Danny is overwhelmed with empathy for him.

Betsy dusts the furniture and windowsills. She does not disturb the olive jar, the socks. She vacuums the carpet, working around the cigarette ashes. Her behavior is a mystery to her. A greater puzzle is the absence of her anger. She orders pizza, leaves two congealed slices in the box, and abandons it on top of the television. After five weeks, the sheets on the sofa bed remain unchanged.

Danny scours the apartment bathtub with Ajax. He knocks over a cup of coffee on the kitchen counter and lets the spill stay there, sticky with cream and sugar. A crowd of tiny flies is attracted to the mess. He leaves the entire Sunday *New York Times* spread around the base of the toilet. He envisions grubby sex with Betsy amid the squalor.

Betsy fails to empty the garbage. Danny fails to scrape an exploded frozen dinner from the walls of the microwave. Betsy leaves globs of toothpaste in the bathroom sink. Danny leaves his boxer shorts and undershirt in a pile by the television.

The kids' house is pristine. Danny uses quantities of hot water and a scrub brush to wash the concrete front porch. With a toothpick, Betsy scrapes accumulated cooking grease from visually inaccessible crevices under the oven hood. Twelve days pass before she realizes the bodyworker hasn't called.

On a Wednesday night at the kids' house, after Meghan and Jason are asleep, Betsy opens the drawer on Danny's side of the bed and finds the cowboy's wristwatch. It isn't even hidden under anything. She sits on the edge of the bed for ninety minutes, then falls over onto Danny's pillow and breathes him in. For the rest of the week she sleeps on his side of the bed, and when Danny comes home to the kids' house on Sunday night from the fetid studio, he stays up late, agitated. The smell of her is on his pillow. The watch is no longer in his drawer. He cannot sleep.

At two o'clock in the morning, there is a knock on the studio apartment door. Betsy looks through the peephole. She is sweating from the exertion of housework. Outside, Danny stands on the threshold, a child asleep on each shoulder. Betsy pauses, breathes, grips the doorknob. Behind her, the apartment gleams.

the necessity of certain behaviors

t o escape from the hot city and the people in it, Lisa goes on an ecotourism trek in the mountains of a foreign country. To get there she endures a long airplane ride. There is the usual business of camping equipment and protein bars and local guides in odd headgear carrying packs containing tea and dried meat. But one afternoon she becomes separated from her group of Americans, and after trudging half a day on a narrow path that doesn't look all that well-traveled, she comes to a village.

Lisa is thirsty, and relieved to have stumbled across civilization. She spent the last hour considering the possibility that when night fell, the mountain goats could become aggressive. She'd read a novel set in Wyoming in which a wild sheep attacks a tourist on a motorcycle. She is teary and grateful when a woman comes out of a hut and gives her a bowl with water in it. With a great deal of kindness the woman watches her drink, and then takes her by the hand. She brings Lisa into the hut and feeds her a stew of meat and a starchy root vegetable, flavored with sweet spices and featuring pleasant pungency caused, Lisa guesses, by someone having aged, or possibly smoked, a key ingredient. She thinks of a wedge of stinky cheese dredged in honey and almonds that someone brought to an office party.

Their stools sit six inches off the dirt floor. Lisa smiles and points at the food. She flashes a thumbs-up to the woman, who clearly doesn't understand. The woman is young, about Lisa's age, with muscular arms. She has a straight long nose and black eyes and moves with economy around her little hut. The woman points to a mat on the floor and Lisa removes her two hundred-dollar hiking boots and falls asleep.

When she wakes up it is still dark, and the woman is at the other side of the hut. She is washing herself, sitting cross-legged on an animal-skin rug with a bowl of water in front of her. A single candle burns, illuminating her brown body. It occurs to Lisa that the woman might know she's being watched.

In the city where she's from, Lisa knew a man named Bennett with full Greek eyelids, a cynical urban grin, and unappeasable curiosity about Lisa's feelings. Some mornings while she showered they'd pretend she wasn't aware he was watching her through the vinyl curtain, which was clear but tinted a flattering pink. Her selection of the curtain was deliberate. In the city where she is from, people in love understand the necessity of certain behaviors.

The woman's name is unpronounceable, but Lisa tries: "Hee-nara?" she says. Now, in the morning, there is another woman in the hut, someone who appears to have stopped by for the purpose of staring. Her hair has been braided and piled on top of her head in a complicated arrangement. She wears a red cowboy shirt and a skirt made of a soft animal skin. She and Heenara sit with thighs touching, talking in low voices and looking at Lisa. They seem to be very close, like sisters. The woman leans over and deposits a long kiss on Heenara's lips. Lisa realizes she was wrong about the sister thing. They look at Lisa, apparently for a reaction. To put them at ease, she smiles.

Heenara and her girlfriend take Lisa for a walk in the village. People emerge from their huts and look at her. Each hut seems to contain only one person. Everyone is young and robust-looking. All in all, this is a very attractive tribe, or clan, or whatever.

In the parlance of the city where she lived, Lisa does not "identify" as bisexual. She is a straight girl who on occasion will take a woman home. After having spent some time in her early twenties thinking about the issue, she settled on refusing to label herself.

This train of sexual thought has not rumbled unprovoked into Lisa's head. Heenara has received another visitor, this time a man, who, like the other men of the village, walks around bare-chested and has a shiny mane of black hair. With this guy Heenara repeats the show of kissing. They take a break and regard Lisa, who offers what she believes to be an encouraging expression. Heenara throws back her head and laughs. Her neck is both soft and muscular. The man's name sounds something like Luck. He smiles brilliantly when she tries to pronounce it. Lisa wonders how he keeps his teeth so white.

The villagers are exceptionally good cooks. Lisa sees no children and no old people. Their language sounds like a stream over stones.

Lisa becomes the village guest. She spends a night or two in the huts of a dozen different people, each cheerful and attentive. One afternoon, she is helping her latest host prepare a batch of root stew and it occurs to her to wonder whether anyone has been feeding her dog. His name is Digit and he's a fairly good-natured animal, considering the fact that he lives in a six-hundred-square-foot box five stories above the ground. The man named Bennett had been particularly fond of him. If he could speak, Digit would be the kind of dog who wouldn't mind being pressed to reveal information, at any given moment, about his current state of mind.

If the villagers experienced curiosity about Lisa, it now appears to be satisfied. Although the language barrier is undoubtedly a factor in their failure to inquire where she's from, Lisa suspects that even if she could talk with them freely, they would not be particularly interested about her place of origin or whether she plans to return. Their unconditional acceptance feels both welcoming and indifferent, like a warm hug from an uncle who keeps forgetting your name. But what would be the point of going home? Only twenty or so people will have even noticed she's gone, if you count her coworkers, her doorman, and the super. Back home, Lisa failed to work toward establishing a circle of friends, a practice that seems important to other city dwellers. Here in the village, a community has made itself available to her, with practically no effort on her part. Sticking around feels logical, plus the people are sexy.

She makes Heenara understand, through a comic series of gestures, that she's evolved past the guest phase and wants a hut of her own. Twenty villagers show up to build it for her. There is no mention of how or whether Lisa will pay for building materials, which mostly consist of mud and fronds and such. During construction they sing slow, melodic songs in a companionable harmony. An unusually tall woman with a high forehead teaches Lisa how to weave her roof from strands of ropy grass. In two days the hut is finished, and people come by with gifts for her: a rug, some wool for her mattress, a candle. The emergency supplies in her backpack now seem foreign and useless: waterproof matches, freeze-dried chicken noodle soup, a flare gun.

One night, Heenara and Luck drop by for a visit. Heenara has been crying. Drawing stick figures in the dirt floor, Heenara explains that she and the woman with complicated hair are no longer together. Luck makes a sympathetic face and puts his arm around Heenara's shoulder. Lisa is impressed with his ability to conceal his pleasure at this development. She serves them bowls of a fermented plum beverage brought as a housewarming present. They pass the time attempting to teach Lisa more of their impossible language and after they're all fairly drunk, Lisa draws two stick figures in her dirt floor meant to represent Heenara and Luck. She puts a circle around the two figures, and smiles at Luck. She reaches for their hands and clasps them together, pantomiming something like, Now you have Heenara all to yourself!

Heenara looks at Luck. They frown at one another and exchange a series of rapid sentences. She shakes her head and glances sideways at Lisa.

Luck picks up the stick. He draws, outside the circle Lisa has made but standing next to his own image, a figure of a man. He points at that figure and pronounces a name that sounds as if he's trying to say "Frederick" with a mouthful of stones. He draws another circle, now around this new man and himself, and overlapping Heenara's. Luck stands in the overlap of the two circles. Lisa smiles politely at the dirt diagram and raises her eyebrows. Heenara makes an exasperated sound. She draws a figure of the woman with complicated hair, next to her own image, and then a circle that encompasses the two of them, but not Luck. She pauses to see if Lisa understands. Then she erases the figure of her ex-girlfriend, leaving a blank space. She holds her two hands out to Lisa. She smiles at her left hand, which is cupped, as if holding something, and nods toward Luck. She shrugs sadly at the other, whose fingers are splayed open, empty.

Lisa takes a swallow of the plum wine. In the blank space left by the woman with complicated hair, she draws a woman with a backpack. Luck ducks his head, grinning into his wine. He kisses them both on the cheek and leaves the hut.

Heenara keeps her awake until sunrise. She performs a ritual involving a paste made of wine mixed into palmful of dirt gathered from under

Lisa's sleeping mat. She hums a soulful tune and nakedly dances a series of steps around Lisa's front door. She removes Lisa's clothes and washes her with maternal tenderness from head to toe using a latherless soap that leaves an oily film and smells like oregano and fruit nectar. Finally she hoists Lisa over her shoulder like a sack, drops her ungently onto the sleeping mat, and pours the remaining wine over her torso, her legs, her shoulders and arms. They slide together with the wine as lubricant until it becomes sticky, whereupon Lisa demonstrates with her mouth one or two cleansing rituals commonly practiced among a tribe of humans she used to know.

When Heenara is asleep, Lisa stands in the open doorway. The stars above the village crowd the sky. How could there possibly be room for them all, she thinks. How is it that they don't smash into each other in chaotic collisions of light and heat?

In the flat tones of their urban language, the man Bennett told her he was building a three-bedroom house in Westchester for himself and a woman named Julie. He said he admired Julie's devotion to transparency. Lisa's relationship with Bennett had long since ended; there was no particular reason for him to tell her all this. Still, months after he moved away from the city Lisa carried on interior dialogues with the memory of him. It was to be expected that he'd have identified someone new, but nevertheless the matter of Julie had startled her. Since her arrival in the village she hasn't had a single imaginary conversation with him.

Lisa wakes up at dawn to Heenara pushing her gently off the mat. She accepts a bowl of hot tea. As soon as she's standing, Heenara pulls the mat from the floor and lays it outside, in the dirt. The plum wine has left a stain in the outline of Lisa's body. Heenara sips tea in the yard. Villagers appear. They approach, smiling, slapping Heenara on the back and raising their eyebrows in the direction of Lisa's door. Through the cracks in the wall, Lisa watches.

A caravan of donkeys led by a couple of men in odd headgear arrives in the village. They pull packs off the animals and open their contents, spreading a blanket on the ground and displaying aluminum cookware, athletic socks, sewing needles. Lisa would like to have a necklace made of carved bone beads, but has nothing with which to trade. There was a time when she would purchase beautiful things. A set of vintage turquoise martini glasses. A distressed calfskin briefcase with copper buckles. Jade earrings set in Balinese silver. She waits for a feeling of longing to occur but the memory of these items is akin to a foreign object in her eye. How silly she used to be!

One of the traders stares at her. Heenara says something sharp to him and he turns away.

The opening weeks of her relationship with Heenara are spent in a sexual frenzy broken up only by Heenara's perfunctory visits to Luck's hut. Upon her return Lisa smells him on Heenara's skin, which she finds not unpleasant. Beating her mat clean on the rocks at the stream, Lisa runs into him. He's polite but has a pained look that suggests his patience is wearing thin. She learns from Heenara that Luck's lover Frederick is away from the village with a group of hunters, tracking a herd of mountain goats across the plateau.

One evening Luck appears at her door. He's had a fair amount of plum wine. Her remedial knowledge of their language results in a distressing conversation in which she understands that Luck wants her to break up with Heenara. When he sees Lisa's tears he leaves and returns with Heenara, who rolls her eyes in the direction of the sheepish Luck and informs Lisa via their semi-efficient system of communication that it's time for Lisa to find a boyfriend.

Among the village inhabitants there is a specialist in such matters. She visits Lisa's hut and cheerfully submits her to a series of questions Lisa only halfway understands, having mostly to do with matters such as eyes, hair, and body type. She strikes Lisa as being awfully young for the job. Lisa defers to her judgment about borrowing a dress that displays her cleavage, and together they spend the following morning visiting a handful of potential boyfriends. Each of them is beautiful beyond belief. Their upper bodies trigger a hazy memory of men lifting weights in a gym located in the gay section of the city where she used to live. The men look at her as though she were some exquisite yet puzzling object they uncovered while digging a hole.

She finds herself judging them by the way they move around their huts. She finally settles on one whose name she mispronounces less comically than the others and who betrays his nervousness by splashing a bit of boiling water on his foot in the process of making her a cup of bitter tea. He's called Toruk, more or less, and she finds herself flirting uncontrollably with him, as if overcome by some Darwinian instinct to snag a hunter-gatherer of her own.

In the days following Bennett's revelations about Julie and Westchester, Lisa experienced an accelerated interest in her psyche by certain people in her life. Her mother; a previously indifferent coworker; her gay boyfriend. They grilled her regarding what had occurred between her and Bennett and what had not; what was said and what was left unsaid. They berated her for her failure to expose herself, as is apparently standard practice in the pursuit of modern urban love. Such a fuss, Lisa thinks now. How did she endure it? Why didn't she leave the city so much earlier?

In preparation for her date with Toruk, Heenara coaches Lisa on the first-night ritual, the initiation of which turns out to be the responsibility of the aggressor, in this case Lisa. Teaching her the steps to the front-door dance and the nonsensical lyrics of the song that accompanies it, Heenara becomes teary and in need of assurance. Or maybe Heenara is preoccupied with something she can't translate—crop failure, or perhaps a sick parent. Which would constitute a mystery in itself, Lisa realizes: she still hasn't encountered any old people. Heenara and Lisa get very drunk and make bittersweet, dramatic love until Lisa gets out of bed to vomit in the bushes behind her hut.

In the morning she awakes to voices in the front yard. She goes outside. Heenara is talking to the trader who came to the village and stared at Lisa. She uses words Lisa more or less understands to explain the man has said that people in the town at the base of the mountain are asking about a woman with yellow hair. "A woman who is lost," she says.

Lisa shakes her head and says something like, "Not lost, me." Heenara smiles.

The man has brown teeth. He lets loose a current of words. He gestures in Lisa's direction. Heenara raises her voice and flaps her hand, shooing him from the yard. Lisa goes inside and pulls the hiking boots from her backpack. She runs after the man and gives them to him. She looks him carefully in the face.

"Not lost, me," she says.

He takes the boots and nods. He doesn't meet her eye. Surely he understands, though, about payment for complicity. Lisa walks back to her hut. The trader will sell her boots for a nice amount of money. He'll feed his family for a month.

In the city at the bottom of the mountain there are probably people looking for her, probably paid by her mother. It's not too late to chase the trader. To erase any ambiguity regarding her desire for his silence. She should appeal to his love of homeland, his indigenous understanding that this is the place, not her city, where humans are meant to live.

Heenara has seen the exchange. She frowns, and goes inside. Slung by their laces over the trader's shoulder, Lisa's boots retreat down the mountain. She tries to make Heenara understand. But she lacks the words to explain that she no longer knows the difference between *lost* and *found*.

For the occasion of their first night together, Toruk has shaved his beard. As part of this procedure he has applied to the skin of his face a berry-scented oil that reminds Lisa of a sweet drink she often consumed as a child. He remains still, waiting for her to move toward him, and when she arrives at his bare chest he raises his arms as if to offer his underbelly. She reaches up to pull on his biceps, to place his arms around her waist, but he refuses to move them. She pulls harder, and he smiles at her and shakes his head. If necessary she could hang the entire weight of her body on these arms.

She performs the ritual to the best of her ability. Toruk smiles understandingly when she screws up the dance and also skips an entire verse of the song. In the washing of his skin she finds herself in a trance of sorts, focused and consumed by the task, unbothered by a soap that won't yield suds. She becomes giggly when the time comes for her to toss him into bed, unsure how to approach the feat of physically moving a mountain of muscle, but he solves the problem by throwing himself onto the mat with what appears to be a painful thud.

She pours the wine on him. Finally, he abandons his ritual passivity and pulls her sharply to the floor to land hard on his body, very nearly knocking her breath away. She is thrilled by the jolt of it, and by her own desire: she found it so rarely in the city.

In the morning she sleeps late. When she wakes up, Toruk is glaring at her. She's forgotten to display the stained mat in his front yard. She's forgotten to receive congratulatory visitors. She doesn't know how to say I'm sorry in his language. She pouts in a shamefaced way and sucks his dick by way of apology.

Sometimes the man named Bennett used to step inside the shower. In the pink light he'd wash her hair. He'd ask if she was okay. When he performed these tender acts she was careful to maintain a neutral expression. Since her face was already wet she could cry without provoking questions as long as she kept her lip from trembling. She didn't want to explain her happiness to him. The joy she harbored was so easily scared away.

Heenara retreats to Luck's sleeping mat to wait out Lisa's infatuation with Toruk. After only two days, however, Frederick returns from the hunt, triumphant with goat meat and horny for Luck. Lisa is at the village well when the hunters return. Luck dashes across the dusty compound to slam into Frederick's body, their mouths joining in a display of sweaty lust. Everyone stops to watch.

Lisa runs into Heenara outside the shower hut. She cups her neck affectionately, but Heenara is stiff. Lisa pulls her by the hair into a stall and closes the woven straw curtain. She turns the warm water on their bodies and methodically works half her hand into Heenara's vagina. This, it turns out, was the right thing to do. Heenara is smug and satisfied.

Lisa finds herself unable to apply to her new life the wisdoms she knew in the old. For example: don't meet the eyes of strangers. Don't be tempted to take the local train; sit tight for the express. Walk at night to the Laundromat with your pepper spray ready, however do feel free to yell at men pissing against your building: no one with a limp penis in his hand is a threat. Expect that all lovers, eventually, will leave.

Lisa comes to the realization that on any given night, one-third of the huts in the village are empty. She speculates on the efficiency, resource-wise, of this arrangement. She wonders if this condition is related to the eerie absence in the village of anyone under the age of eighteen. One night she draws in the dirt floor of Toruk's a hut a stick figure of a small person holding the hand of a larger person. She circles the child figure and says "Where?"

Given Toruk's tender laughter, Lisa's expression must reveal her fear of the question, and of what he might answer. He points to the hills. He talks, he smiles fondly, he says a lot of words. She doesn't need to understand their meaning to know the children have not, after all, been sold into slavery, or sacrificed to some grumpy god.

Slowly, Lisa's comprehension of the stream-over-rocks language gets better. She knows now, for example, that when Toruk looks pensively at the ceiling and utters a masculine yet lilting series of words, he's not making an observation on the vast and mysterious wonders of the universe. As a public works laborer of sorts—preparing communal garden plots, digging sewage canals—he turns out to be mostly preoccupied with moving piles of dirt from one end of the village to another. As for Lisa's own preoccupations, either Toruk doesn't know how to ask or he isn't especially interested.

As time passes, the domino effect created by the prolonged absence of Frederick the goat hunter becomes sorted out. Lisa settles into a routine with Heenara and Toruk. They don't have anything so formal as a schedule of visits, but there emerges between them an understanding that things always even out, more or less.

On a calm morning with huge white clouds in the sky, Bennett arrives in the village, unshaven, dirty, and limping. Behind him is the trader. Filling her water gourd at the well, Lisa spots him before he realizes it's her. When she approaches, he holds her and he cries. "I've been looking for you," he says. He is oblivious to the people staring.

"I'm fine," she says into his shirt. Underneath the old sweat he still smells like Bennett.

Heenara appears, unsmiling, at Lisa's side. Lisa introduces him.

"You speak their language?" Bennett says.

"Not really." She shrugs. She shouldn't be proud of this. "What are you doing here?"

"Your mother is going out of her mind—"

He turns to see why Lisa is looking over his shoulder. Toruk stands at the entrance to his hut, observing them. His arms are folded across his chest. She is surprised to see he's not any taller than Bennett. Heenara removes the water gourd from Lisa's hand and gives it to Bennett for a drink. She takes his arm and walks them to Lisa's hut. She gives Lisa a look and comes inside with them.

"I'm sorry," Lisa says to Bennett.

"What were you thinking?" he says. "Did you lose your passport? Or something? Were you hurt? Are you sick?" He lowers his voice. He watches Heenara. "Are these people keeping you here?"

Heenara is banging around in Lisa's cooking area. Her cheeks are flushed. Lisa is overcome with loyalty toward her. "It's good here," she says.

"You've been living here? In this woman's hovel?" he says.

"Where's Julie?" she asks.

"Home. About ready to leave me over all this." He watches Heenara, who is blowing earnestly on the fire. "What's going on, Lisa?"

"Go back," Lisa says. "Call my mother."

"And tell her what?"

"I don't know. Tell her not to worry."

"Tell me this is a joke," he says. "Is this some kind of joke?"

Bennett pitches an orange pup tent and for two days skulks around the edges of the village. He stakes out Lisa's movements, watching from behind his tent flap. She brings him food, which he accepts wordlessly. The villagers stay clear of him. Apparently they don't know much about stalkers. Lisa's never had one before, and is disappointed hers is so morose and benign.

It becomes colder at night. Toruk presents her with a finely woven goat wool blanket. During an afternoon of cleaning she discovers the backpack in the corner of her hut behind a large pile of wool. She caresses the items inside the pack and thinks about the relative usefulness or frivolity of each. She boils water and prepares the freeze-dried chicken noodle soup. She gives a taste to Heenara, who finds it disgusting.

"I wish you wouldn't spit food on my floor," Lisa says in the stream-over-stones language.

"You call that food?" Heenara says.

Lisa recalls a brunch of salmon benedict and roasted rosemary potatoes at a sidewalk café on the Upper West Side. "I love you," she tells Heenara, although it's possible she's now speaking English.

"I don't understand," Heenara says.

"Neither do I," Lisa replies.

Heenara wipes her thumb across Lisa's forehead, as if to rub out the worry.

Late one afternoon, it snows. The villagers quicken the pace of their work. Many are smiling in a distracted, anticipatory way, lifting their faces to the falling flakes. When it becomes dark, the temperature drops. Lisa approaches Bennett's campsite at the edge of the village and calls his name. He unzips the tent flap, sits back on his heels and gazes up at her.

"Why don't you come inside," she tells him.

"I've been squatting here for three days," Bennett says. "Not much to do."

"It's cold," Lisa says. "I'll heat some stew." She tightens Toruk's blanket around her shoulders.

Bennett stands, stretches his limbs. "I do have a few things to ask you," he says.

The moon is rising with characteristic drama over the eastern mountains. "It's pretty enough," Bennett says after a while. "I can see the appeal."

On the moonlit hillside to the north of the village, a line of people appears, making its way down the path. Lisa and Bennett wait for the group to approach. Snow falls thickly, coating rocks, everything.

The travelers are led by a woman with long gray hair and a thin neck. She leans hard on her walking stick, though her pace is steady. The children behind her seem as though they would break into a run if not for a duty to support teetering grandparents. A small group of women follows, carrying babies and toddlers in cloth slings. An ancient man lying in a litter is transported via the muscled shoulders of four very young men. At the rear of the line, attractive teenagers lead pack animals by their halters. Theatrically illuminated by an accommodating moon, the faces in the procession reveal fatigue and communion and anticipation of home.

"Wow," Bennett says. The spectacle passes them by. To the south, Lisa sees villagers wrapped in blankets and waiting in their doorways, each cupping with ritualistic tenderness a steaming bowl of tea. Light from cooking fires behind them creates a series of soft yellow squares on the ground.

From the little hill selected by Bennett three days before for its convenient view of village activity, Lisa witnesses the homecomings. Bennett remains heavily quiet. The boys carrying the old man stop at Toruk's hut and bring him inside. At Heenara's door, one of the women with an infant sling removes the baby from its pouch and hands it, squalling, to her. Their heads are thrown back in laughter. Together they drink from the bowl of tea. At each hut, couples reassemble. One at a time the doors close, until every yellow square is extinguished.

Bennett sets his arm across Lisa's shoulders and guides her down the path to her hut. In the warm interior he ladles her stew into bowls. Through the walls of grass and mud comes the muted gurgle of families in conversation.

acknowledgments

These stories previously appeared in the following journals, sometimes in slightly different form:

American Literary Review ("Housework"); *American Short Fiction* ("The Steam Room"); *Colorado Review* ("Juniper Beach"); *Massachusetts Review* ("This Is How It Starts," "The Queer Zoo"); *New England Review* ("The Necessity of Certain Behaviors"); *Southwords* ("The Nigerian Princes"); *Tin House* ("Cultivation").

"The Necessity of Certain Behaviors" appeared in *The O. Henry Prize Stories 2008*.

"Cultivation" appeared in the *Pushcart Prize XXXIII*.

I am grateful for my teachers: Karen Brennan, Rob Cohen, Meg Files, Kit McIlroy, Jim Shepard, and Pete Turchi. I am grateful for the institutions that have grown me as a writer and all the fine folks who keep them going: Pima Community College, The Program for Writers at Warren Wilson College, Bread Loaf Writers' Conference, the National Endowment for the Arts, Tucson Pima Arts Council, the Arizona Commission on the Arts, and the Tucson Historic Warehouse Arts District.

I am grateful for the writers and friends who have given their loving, intelligent attention to these stories and to their author: Charlie Buck, Maureen Cain, Lucy Corin, Stacey D'Erasmo, Ben George, Judith Grossman, Elinor Lipman, Ted Robbins, Christine Schutt, and especially the wise and steadfast Robin Black. I am grateful for Kore Press and for Lisa Bowden, separately and together.

I am grateful for these stories, for helping me learn perseverance and humility. I am grateful for the editors of the fine literary magazines who first gave them a home. I am grateful for the vision and generosity of Drue Heinz, for the caring and heroically patient people at University of Pittsburgh Press, for Alice Mattison, and for my dear agent, Sarah Burnes.

I am grateful for my students. I am grateful for eleven years of love and support from Karin Uhlich. I am grateful for my family, for Tucson, and for Brennan.